Forks in the Flowerpots

by
JoJo Schroeder

Blue Mustang Press
Boston, Massachusetts

First printing

ISBN 978-0-9759737-5-2
PUBLISHED BY BLUE MUSTANG PRESS
www.BlueMustangPress.com
Boston, Massachusetts

Printed in the United States of America

Dedication

To my real-life muse, whose ability to lean in a manner calculated to drive young girls wild inspired all sorts of creative thoughts at a very early age.

Forks in the Flowerpots

Chapter 1

The October sun beamed down on Mr. Cabbot's balding head. The prolonged sunny weather, the changing trees, the molding leaves, the pungent earth, these were the sights and smells of one of the more colorful, fragrant New England falls he had ever witnessed. Yet to him all the beauty and aroma only served to stimulate histamine. Mr. Cabbot had been warring with his allergies for three weeks now. He sniffed loudly to thrust the mucus back up his nasal passage. The thick secretion traveled swiftly toward his esophagus but was diverted by a severe hacking relocating it in his mouth. He spit it out onto the sidewalk.

"Shit." He mumbled. Besides these friggin' allergies the video store wasn't doing good business right now. It was the new store down the street putting him out of work. All these new chains and their new selections and their new look.

Mr. Cabbot turned to step back into his store. Enough loafing. He heard a car door slam and glanced across the street in time to see Janice Elderby ascending the church steps. He watched her graceful backside swing gently to and fro as she trotted forward, head in the air, shoulders back, well aware of her allure. Mr. Cabbot appreciated the view of a good-looking woman from behind. He appreciated it very much. He didn't particularly like Janice, but he sure could appreciate her from behind. And he knew that other people appreciated her from behind as well. Today she was headed to church. Mr. Cabbot grunted softly.

"So Father Dillard is diddling a new one." He smiled slyly. "Man's been here no more than three months now and already he's on number two."

He shook his head. "I shoulda taken up theology."

Janice Elderby tried to focus on the back wall of the inside of the confessional. Her movement was rhythmic and slow, and she had to concentrate to keep from moaning aloud as John Dillard aggressively kneaded her small breasts. "Push harder, John. Hold me down against you. Yeah, like that." Janice's whispers were barely audible and breathless.

It was with difficulty that Father Dillard did as he was told. Any other woman and he would have insisted on a less impeding location than the confessional in his church for an encounter, but Janice was his most erotic daydream coming true and as he had told his visiting cousin last week, "for a chance at her cunt in my mouth I'd risk even this." It was a long coveted position he finally held, a small town in New England not too far from Boston.

Janice bent over him suddenly and bit gently into his ear to stifle an escaping grunt.

John felt her exhale in his ear. The heat of her breath traveled down his neck. The blood rushed to his genitals. He grabbed Janice's hips and held her still.

"Don't move. Don't move." He hissed.

Janice gasped. Her words, though barely audible, were urgent. "Now, John."

John's face contorted into an intense scowl before he buried his face into Janice's shoulder. One moment of complete stillness: no breathing, no movement.

They rocked gently together and took their first breath.

Janice brushed her hand lightly across the back of her pleated skirt as she alighted from the church threshold into the autumn afternoon. Her strong calves made her fashionably heeled pumps click impertinently on the stone steps. Her pace was more sedate than her thoughts. She was late picking up Daniella from day-care, but to rush might dislodge some of the slowly retreating sperm and since Janice no longer wore underwear to church she risked the trickle of unaccepted semen down her leg. It was only on the last two occasions that John hadn't worn a condom. It was unwise, Janice mused. Maybe she'd get a disease. One she couldn't explain to Doug.

Janice started up her car. A disease that some charity clinic would tell her about in complete confidentiality, advising and cajoling her as if she were one of their pathetic, pimply, teenage clientele. She shook her head and smirked. So what.

This affair with John was the only thing that kept her ticking day in and day out. It was what allowed her to listen to Doug's banter, give parties, host dinners, listen to teachers, help with homework, organize inept do-gooders, and smile, smile, smile. It helped her get up in the morning and fall asleep at night.

It was meaningless. But no more meaningless than every thing else. And the sex was good. The orgasms were good. It was reckless; they were doing it in the church. What the hell, it was erotic and she liked thinking about it.

When she sat on his lap facing him they just fit in the dark, musty, confessional. The confessional would quickly smell of sex, which John liked. Orgasm was bitter-sweet for Janice. She had to fight the urge to cry out, but that added to the excitement. This was control. This was Janice calling the shots, running her life, carrying around a shameful secret and being delighted by her other life. *Now* the North Brooktown women had reason to envy her.

She had always inspired envy, for as long as she could remember. And envy had always kept her somewhat apart. North Brooktown was no different than prep school, and Houston and College and Amherst. But she was envied for all the wrong reasons. The thirty-something women of North Brooktown's society envied her youthful beauty and slender figure, even after two children, whereas the young, horny, teenage girls envied her marriage to her handsome, stereotypical New England professor-husband, who taught at Amherst College. The newly married women envied her ability to do it all. But despite her accomplishments as mother and wife and all the self-fulfillment, pop-psych books Janice had thumbed through, she was lonely and restless and sinking into an abyss of emptiness. John Dillard's childlike willingness to fulfill her fantasies gave her control. It gave her power. This was her release, her rebellion. And what a powerful aphrodisiac this control made. Sex had never before been this good.

Bruce and Dan reclined lazily on Bruce's front yard, picking at red and yellow leaves and letting the uncommonly warm autumn sun pour over them.

Dan was beginning to feel impatient. He wasn't an impatient person by nature, but he'd heard so much about this woman, how different she appeared to be, what a nice ass she had, how cute she was, that he was getting anxious to see her.

They'd been watching her house for a good half-hour now and no sign of the object of Bruce's infatuation.

Dan turned to his friend. "How do you know she's even home?"

"That's her car." Bruce pointed to the beat up white Toyota in the driveway of the house catty corner and on the other side of the street from where they sat.

Suddenly he sat upright. "Oh shit, there she is!"

Dan barely had a chance to glance over at the woman coming out of her house before he noticed that Bruce had bounded up and was rounding the corner of his own house and out of sight.

Dan watched her for a moment as she walked down the street in the opposite direction. He didn't care enough to wonder where she might be going, but he thought she did indeed have a nice ass. Other than that he saw a youngish looking woman wearing jeans and a blue sweater with light brown hair, blondish maybe. She wasn't beautiful or breathtaking. Pretty ordinary actually.

Dan found Bruce behind the house stocking the woodpile.

"What happened to you?" He asked.

"I panicked."

"You panicked? Does she know you from Jesus?"

"I talked to her once."

"Yeah, you gave her directions, pal. That isn't exactly forming a bond, you know."

"Hey, I'm trying to get her to notice me. It's fucking hard. But I'm working on it."

"You took off! You bolted to the back of the house. You call that working on it?"

Bruce grimaced. "Up yours."

Dan dropped his hand on his friend's shoulder.

"I haven't seen you this stupid since that day you met Terri, back in ninth grade. That was seven years ago."

"I can count."

"I wonder what Jen'll say to this."

"You don't have to tell her, Dan."

"Are you kidding? Your love life is more important to Jen than ours."

"Great."

Ella walked toward the graveyard. She knew exactly where she was going. As small and unknown as North Brooktown was, she had been here before, with Chris. They had sat together in that graveyard in the October sun, almost exactly one year ago, on the autumn leaves under the trees.

North Brooktown was the stereotype Ella wouldn't have believed existed until she stood in the thick of it. Chris had brought her here on their vacation because it had been his home once.

Ella flopped onto her back and stared at the clouds. She'd wanted to come back here since she left. Now she was here. She sighed. Half the attraction of North Brooktown had been that Chris had lived here and had loved it. At least, in retrospect that had been half the attraction. Being here without him made her ache for his company even more than she had anticipated.

It was as pretty and charming as it had been last year. Ella was painfully aware of the golden, flame-red, and burnt orange leaves on the trees, changing ever so slightly every day.

"So what?" She mumbled to herself. "So the hell what!"

Beauty, when you're heartbroken, is depressing.

Chapter 2

"If she is moving here, where's the moving van, or the U-haul?" Dan asked.

"She's been here two weeks. If she's not living here what the hell is she doing here?" Bruce pointed out.

"What the hell are *we* doing here anyway?"

It wasn't that Dan objected to sitting on the bench along Main Street. The weather was still defying all weather predictions with 70 degrees and sunshine and brilliant leaves. But this particular sit felt purposeful and Dan thought he was entitled to enlightenment.

"She takes a walk almost every afternoon when she gets home and she usually comes this way."

"Gets home from where?"

"I don't know, but we get home about the same time and I've seen her walk down this street after changing clothes. Four times in the last week."

"You're sick, man. You know spying on some one is a felony or something."

"I'm not spying. I see her go in her door all dressed up, I see her come out in jeans, I see her walk down the street."

Dan mused for a moment and then asked, "what about Megan?"

"What about her?"

"Does she know you're spying on some school teacher?"

"What school teacher?"

Bruce looked at his friend. Dan smiled.

"How do you know she's a school teacher?" Bruce was suddenly upright and interested. "Is that what she is? A school teacher?"

Dan nodded. "Yep. Teaches in Brooktown at the middle school. My mom saw Mrs. Wassermann at Ames or something and

I guess her son is in Ms. *Sinclair's* class." He said her name with a drawl.

Bruce stared down Summer Street. After awhile he said, "What's her first name?"

"Ella."

Bruce sat with a far away grin on his face and said quietly, "Ella Sinclair."

Janice stared at the invitations she was addressing. Ugh, the Ellis'. What god-awful people, she thought. Their daughter's nose was always noticeably running with a big glob of yellow-green mucus resting threateningly in her left nostril. Did she ever blow it?

Doug let the door swing shut intruding on her thoughts. "Hello?"

"In here." She responded from their elegant dining room.

"Hi pet." He laid a hand on her shoulder as he passed her on his way to the kitchen.

Doug. Her husband. Had she ever been in love with him? Did she even love him? Did it matter? Janice shook the thought from her head. Why wonder now?

Doug was asking her about her day. It was the same routine every day. He asked and she would mention a few of the details and then return the greeting. He would talk about a few of the "stupider" students in his classes and some of their insipid questions. Or he'd complain about the faculty politics; the pressure he was under. Then he'd grab the newspaper and ask about dinner. Janice would return to whatever task with which she was currently occupied. And so would pass their days into oblivion. It used to make her unbelievably sad. And in the beginning she tried to remedy it. But as she became more and more of a wife and mother she became less and less of herself. After twelve years she didn't exist anymore, not as Janice. She had become Mrs. Elderby. Mom.

She returned her attention to the invitations. John Dillard. The next one went to Father John Dillard. She smiled. She could smile about her secret. No one was watching. Except Mr. Cabbot. Janice frowned when she recalled his lewd smile yesterday as she paid for her son's video rental. It was only surprising because it was the first time he had directed his attentions at her. Until yesterday he had maintained a sort of reverence. Why so bold now? She shuddered slightly at his portly, balding, sparsely-toothed countenance. Then she smiled and started writing again. Her secret was making her slightly paranoid. How delicious.

Jason Elderby stood looking intently at the drama section. It was a feigned interest, obvious to those who knew what to look for. He stared relentlessly at the same video jacket, stealing suspicious glances around the shop when he thought no one was looking.

Mr. Cabbot threw a look in his direction. That boy! He spent more time watching videos than any kid his age should. He should be out runnin' around with his friends. But he never was out running around. And he didn't seem to have any friends, at least none that ever came in the store with him, and little Elderby came into the store a lot. Cabbot shook his head. There he was pretending to read the cover of "Time is forever" again. He should have it memorized by now. Jesus, the kids these days. Nothin' but trouble.

"Time is forever" was in the drama section which was connected to the adult area and if he stood at the very edge of the drama videos he could just see one panel of the sex videos. Jason's imagination worked over-time to fill in the censored areas. He'd already seen pictures of nipples and pubic hair in Tad Johnson's Penthouse. Tad Johnson and Jimmy Ballenheimer were lucky. They had dirty magazines and cable TV and their moms worked, so they could do whatever they wanted after school. Jason knew that first hand. One time Jimmy Ballenheimer had invited Jason to watch the Playboy channel with them after school. Jason had refused. Jimmy laughed at him and told him to go on home; he was too young anyway. Jimmy and Tad were 14. Jason would be 11 in four months. Jason hadn't cared about the Playboy channel and Penthouse magazine back then. He'd just been flattered that he'd received an invitation to spend time with two other boys. The last time he'd been invited anywhere was in third grade when Sally Sutherland asked him to come to her birthday party. But that was before. Now he couldn't stop thinking about the pictures he'd seen. But his imagination was limited. He needed a resource. Maybe Jimmy or Tad would invite him over again. He really wanted to watch the Playboy channel now. He really wanted to look through a "Penthouse". The desire to see those pictures made him feel guilty.

If his parents knew they would be disgusted.

Jason turned away from the videos. He felt evil. He kept his head down and left the store.

Bruce turned his car onto Summer Street from Elm. He had taken the long way home today. He wanted to just spend time today. Think about things. Dream about Ella.

He was pulling up to his house as Ella was pulling up to hers. He climbed slowly out of his old Chevy. There she was. Right there. It took her a moment to notice him leaning slightly against his car watching her. When her gaze met his, his heart jumped. Shit. She was looking at him. And what's more, she had caught him staring at her. Just as Bruce started to shift his glance and move away he caught a glimpse of Ella waving. He looked at her. She waved again. He grinned and held up a hand.

Emboldened, Bruce crossed the street. Ella was busy pulling pieces of an old ten-speed Peugeot out of the trunk of her car.

"Need some help?" Bruce offered.

"You wouldn't happen to know how to piece together a bicycle, would you?"

"I'm practically professional."

"Is that what you're doing when you're not parked on the Main Street benches?"

Bruce smiled a little.

"I've seen you, with your friend, sitting there sometimes." Ella said.

"Yeah, I've seen you too."

Ella stuck out her hand. "Well then. Hi. I'm Ella Sinclair."

Bruce shook her hand. "Yeah."

Ella raised her eyebrows. "Yeah?"

Bruce grinned. "Yeah. Ella's a good name for you. Perfectly appropriate."

"Mm, well, thank you. I'd like to say the same."

"Bruce Hurowitz."

"Ah, yes. Definitely. Very you."

It wasn't long before the bicycle was pieced together successfully except for the peddles which were no where to be found. They agreed that the bike was of little value without peddles, but it was stored in the shed anyway, and Bruce accepted Ella's offer of "Coffee or something".

Bruce glanced around at Ella's empty house.

"Where's the furniture?"

Ella pointed to the corner by the fireplace. "There's a lamp."

"Oh, right. What else do you need?"

"O.K. smarty pants, I happen to have a bed and a laundry basket too."

"A laundry basket is key."

"Well, I keep my crocheting in it."

"Me too."

"Shut up."

"What you've got here is negative space. Minimalism is in."

"Thanks for the commentary Mr. Interior Decorator. I just moved here, you know."

"Yeah, I know. And we're glad of it."

"Oh, are we?"

Bruce nodded largely.

He nodded toward the front room. "If you get tired of the echo I know some good thrift stores in the area."

"Ah, you put your finger on the pulse, friend. Thrift stores are what I need. Good ones. Quaint."

"Quaint. You got it."

"So, when?"

"When?"

"When do we go to these thrift stores?"

"Wednesday evening?"

"You don't have anything better to do on Wednesday evening than take me to a thrift store?"

"'Better' is a subjective term, Ms. Sinclair. I'm wishing it were Tuesday night."

"Lucky me. I guess Wednesday it is, then. C'mon the coffee's in the kitchen."

Bruce watched Ella as she poured the hot water over the grounds in the plastic filter.

"You must not get a whole lot of coffee drinking company." He commented.

"Why do you say that?"

16

"Cuz if you had to make six people coffee that way guest number one's coffee would be stone cold by the time you finished the cup for guest number five."

Ella smirked at him. "Will you give me a break? I just moved here. Besides, it tastes better this way."

"You like teaching better here than in California?"

Ella glanced up surprised at the sudden change in topic. "How do you know I teach? And how do you know I'm from California?"

"Small town."

"Uh huh." Ella sounded skeptical. "What about you?"

"I go to U Mass. And I work in Worcester part time."

"Wow, sounds like you're busy."

A boyish grin spread across the young man's face.

"I've got some free time."

"Yeah? What's her name?"

"Who's?"

Ella smiled impishly at him as if they shared a secret.

"The woman who makes you smile like that when you're talking about your free time."

Much to his surprise Bruce blushed. He shook his head.

"You've got it all wrong. But when I meet someone you'll be the first to know."

Ella raised her eyebrows.

"You know you look very similar to your mom when you smile."

"I've heard that before."

Ella had met Bruce's mom briefly at the town's one drug store. The woman had introduced herself as Lydia Hurowitz and said, "We're neighbors." Ella remembered seeing the cute kid she had asked directions from in front of Lydia's house and put two and two together. There was familial similarity or Ella might have guessed they were lovers. Of course, Lydia looked 40 at least and the kid was a kid. O.K., "kid" was an understatement. He was a young man. Very young. Eighteen maybe. But eighteen can be just what the doctor ordered when you're 40. So it wasn't a far cry to guess that they were a couple except for the obvious resemblance.

Ella asked Lydia's about her son. It was a favorite subject of Lydia's. Made Ella smile. After fifteen minutes Ella knew more about Bruce than she had ever expected to find out. And he wasn't eighteen, he was twenty-one. And he was cute. Sitting here with him drinking coffee, watching him, hearing his commentary, she had to admit, he was cute. She liked the way he always wore his baseball cap backwards. It made him look mischievous.

They talked for over an hour about autumn, rain, cities verses small towns, dogs as pets, and the medicinal merits of beer. By the time Bruce got up to leave it had grown dark outside and had begun to down-pour. Rain was pounding in sheets against the windows. Ella handed Bruce an umbrella at the door.

"I'm glad we bumped into each other. It's the first time in a while that I've had a nice long chat with someone so easy to talk to."

Bruce leaned against the doorway. "Yeah, it was easy."

He glanced at the umbrella and then leaned it against the wall. He smiled at her. "What, is it raining outside or something?"

Ella smiled back and shook her head.

"I won't need this. I'm right there." He pointed. "Besides," he leaned in toward Ella a bit, "I'm not even gonna feel the rain. Ella."

They stood smiling at each other.

Ella folded her arms across her chest. "Hmm."

"I'll see you Wednesday afternoon."

Ella let the door swing shut and grinned. Stop grinning! He's 21. He's a boy. But he's so sweet, so charming. Ella giggled at his comments about her lack of furniture. He teased so gently. Chris was like that. He reminded her of Chris.

"But he's not Chris." Ella said aloud. Her good mood was stilted. She plopped down on the floor in front of her fireplace and stared gloomily at the cold ashes behind the grate.

Chapter 3

The hands around her little neck tightened and squeezed. They squeezed until her face turned blue and her swollen tongue popped out of her mouth. Then the fumbling fingers pulled up her jeans and zipped them. The red and gold leaves fell around her grotesque body.

Wednesday's weather was heaven sent. Bruce couldn't remember one thing he'd done in lab that morning and he'd delivered the wrong sandwiches to the wrong offices in the afternoon. Somewhere in Worcester an administrative assistant was eating the roast beef sandwich of the dental hygienist who, expecting a roast beef, was doomed to suffering through a Turkey with cheese. But the tedious part of his day had passed and the moment he had been anticipating without interruption was upon him. He was pulling up to Ella's door now with Dan's truck.

Ella looked as ordinary as ever when she answered the door but Bruce was beguiled.

He said, "Nice sweater."

"Thanks. I crocheted it myself."

"Wow." Bruce was suitably impressed.

"Your friend let us use his truck. It's big."

"Yeah. Dan. It's his pride and joy."

"Did you have to promise your first born to get it?"

"He owes me."

Bruce drove them around a thirty-mile radius, taking them into every small town imaginable. Ella was more interested in the beauty of the landscape and coloration than she was in her furniture. In East Brooktown they got out and took a walk. It was Halloween next week and many people in this town took that occasion quite seriously. San Francisco did Halloween, especially in the Castro, but this small-town, decorate-for-a-holiday, mentality was new to her. House after house, shops, restaurants; everyone seemed to have, at the very minimum, a pumpkin on display. She was captivated. New England was "holiday land" to Ella. She tried explaining to Bruce how Halloween and Thanksgiving and Christmas just seemed more authentic when the leaves changed colors, fell from their branches in the cold wind, and were eventually covered by the snow.

"What made you stay in California so long? What was there that you can't find here?"

"On a bitter day in January when I just can't seem to get warm, we'll go over the merits of California. Today, on a day like this, I'm not going to be able to think of any."

Ella glanced at him and then revised, "That's not true. San Francisco is a great city."

"So is Boston." Bruce watched her as she looked around.

"No doubt."

Krim Kram's proprietor moved the old fashioned, heavy, telephone off the table Ella had picked. It was the last thing they loaded on the truck. Her booty included a simple oak desk with two drawers, a darker shaded dresser with deep drawers, the walnut table, (which she got for a steal), and two shabby Victorian chairs. She had fallen in love with each piece. It was a collection of many stores and two hours.

"Perfect!" Ella announced as they fastened the last bungy cord to the side of the truck.

They stood back for a second to admire their work when a screech of tires captured their attention.

A young auburn-haired woman jumped out of the car, pointed at Bruce and yelled, "There you are you lying, cheating, bullshitting, son of a bitch!"

Ella looked at Bruce who was scowling. "I thought you said you didn't have a girlfriend."

The auburn-haired woman stormed over to Bruce. Ella thought she was unusually pretty and wore a lot of eye make up.

"You've got a lot of fucking nerve, Bruce!"

Whether or not all this disturbed him, Bruce played it remarkably calm. Ella was impressed despite herself.

"What's the problem, Meg?"

His even tone seemed to instigate more than soothe.

The auburn-haired woman looked as if she were about to

explode.

"You! You're the goddamn problem! You're a fucking loser, Bruce, and I never want to see your stupid face again!" With that remark she returned noisily to her car and drove off.

Ella grimaced. "Geez, Bruce, I'm sorry."

"Don't be."

They climbed in the truck. Ella waved at the proprietor as they pulled away from the store. He'd watched the whole scene with polite fixation.

"That was Megan Barzoff."

"She's a looker."

"She's not my girlfriend . . ."

Ella interrupted him.

"It's O.K., Bruce, really. It's none of my business."

Bruce smiled. "O.K., Ella. It's none of your business."

"But I hope . . . you know, it's fixable."

He glanced at her. "You do?"

Ella stared out the window. "Sure."

After a moment she said, "You remind me of a friend of mine so much it's uncanny. Sometimes."

"Like now?"

"No. Not now. Not at all. But sometimes."

"A good friend?"

Ella hesitated. "Yes. Once."

"Where is he now?"

"In San Francisco. Why?"

"Is he coming out here?"

Ella looked at him and smiled.

"Is he?" Bruce repeated.

"No. I don't think he's going anywhere."

Bruce pulled up in front of Ella's house. There was half an hour of daylight left with which to unload.

Ella eyed her find as it sat on the sidewalk. "Jesus, Bruce, look at all this. What am I going to do with it when I move?"

"Are you moving?"

"Well, not next month or anything. But, you know ..."

"No. I don't know."

He was staring at her. She stared back, then shook her

21

head.

"Bruce . . . "

"What Ella?"

"Nothing. C'mon, let's take the kitchen stuff inside first."

Arranging the furniture was a short process. And Bruce wasn't shy about putting his two cents in when Ella asked what he thought of this here or that there. When they were finished Ella ordered pizza that they ate at her new table, drank beer and talked.

It was after ten before Bruce said he should be leaving.

Ella walked him to the door. "I really appreciate all this."

"Anytime. I like thrift store shopping with you."

"I didn't mean the thrift store adventure as much as I was referring to having you around. I enjoy your company."

"Yeah, well, I worked pretty hard at being around when you were around. Bumping into you wasn't much of an accident."

"I didn't think so."

Bruce stared at her with a little smile on his lips. He reached for her hand. They both watched in silence as his thumb wandered softly back and forth across the back of her hand.

"Ella, Worcester State's showing "The three Musketeers" Saturday night. The one with Gene Kelly. You wanna . . . "

"Bruce," Ella cut him off, "You're . . . twenty-one."

"I'll be twenty-two next month."

"I'll be twenty-nine."

"Yeah? Happy Birthday. So, you want to go?"

An involuntary grin crept over her face. "I'll let you know."

Thursday morning the Sheriff's Office found Katie Merchant's body. The news spread around North Brooktown and surrounding areas like wild fire. Even the weekly paper went back to the presses to release a supplemental page since it came out Wednesday mornings and the body wasn't reported missing until Wednesday night. The paper told all the details the Sheriff's Office had divulged and speculated on the rest. It was clear that the crime had involved sexual abuse, although to what extent no one really knew, and everyone was trying to figure out.

Ella heard the news from Mr. Cahzo at the Drug store. He was selling a lot of papers that day and suggested Ella buy one while he still had any in stock. He had his own theory about what happened. He thought her Daddy was responsible for the murder. Everyone knew Alwin Merchant was a lech. Ella read the account given to the Town Crier. It said their suspect was probably a small man of below average height. Alwin Merchant was a giant. He might be a lech, Ella thought, but he's a huge lech. The paper mentioned a memorial service, but no date or time. Father Dillard might know.

Ella found Dillard's office near the entrance to the church. No one was answering. She heard a thump from behind her. She walked cautiously toward the pews and confessional. The church was empty. Afternoon light shone through the stained glass windows onto the carpet and alter. It was as tense as it was quiet. Another thump. It sounded muffled. The sound was directly behind her. She swung around and stared at the confessional. To Ella's utter amazement, Mrs. Elderby and Father Dillard emerged from the confessional together, from the *Priest's* portion of the confessional. The three of them stared at each other for a solid minute. Ella suddenly wanted to laugh. She clapped her hand over her mouth so her "Ha" has barely audible. Then she mumbled, "excuse me" and quickly departed.

So. Father Dillard and Janice Elderby . . . well what do you know? Janice Elderby was North Brooktown's society queen. Ella was sure her reign extended a lot further than that, but not being in the same circle she wasn't certain just how much that circle encompassed. And this secret could mean abdication if other society royalty should discover it. Ella started to giggle until she thought of Doug Elderby. Janice had a family. A family that could be hurt very much by this affair. And Ella liked Doug. She'd only met him once, with Janice, when they'd come in to meet their son Jason's new teacher. Doug had been charming and kind. He'd seemed genuinely interested in the curriculum Ella had planned for her classes. But the relationship between the married couple had seemed perfunctory to Ella. It was merely a first impression but it had stuck. They hadn't touched each other at all and neither one seemed to care. They didn't watch one another when the other spoke. There simply seemed to be no interaction. They co-existed as a unit. Ella had seen many couples like that. It seemed that it was merely a matter of time before all relationships reached that point. What was it? Boredom? Even when the relationship started out so well, so in love, somewhere down the line those feelings went away, sometimes quite suddenly, and then there you both were, wondering if you had the strength to split, and the luck to find some one else. Ella shook her head vigorously. Not her. Not Ella. She'd rather search forever, unsuccessfully, than settle for something less than her ideal of love. And she'd thought that her life would be a fairly endless search. So many good relationships had happened to her that to never find one that would last indefinitely didn't seem to be a great sacrifice. Ella saw herself going from one relationship to another until she was too old to care about sex anymore. And then she met Chris. It was different with Chris. It was different right away with Chris. Stop thinking about Chris! Ella yelled at herself.

Ella stomped up her steps and slammed her door. Fucking Chris. He invaded her thoughts. He was everywhere here. What made her think she could ever live here without him? She had just witnessed Janice Elderby screwing Father Dillard in the confessional and all she could think about was Chris!

Ella plopped down on her Victorian chair and put her head in her hands. Little Katie Merchant. Who was Katie Merchant? Ella had never met her. She had only seen her. She did know her older sister, Theresa. Theresa was quiet and withdrawn and a terrible speller. But she'd seen the two of them playing together on the playground one afternoon, and they looked compatible. For sisters, there was a kinship that was surprising. Ella expected sisters to ignore each other every chance they got, but these two seemed to her to gravitate toward each other. They *wanted* to play together. They were united in their seclusion. Yes! That was it. They were united by their loneliness. That was obvious immediately. That was obvious just by watching them interact on the playground. Now there was only Theresa. She was alone in her loneliness because Katie was dead. There was no explanation for why someone killed her. She was dead and would remain dead forever. Suddenly Ella felt tired. She didn't want to think about Katie anymore. Katie Merchant, deceased. Ten years old.

The next day Ella received an invitation from Janice Elderby to join her for Tea at the Green Gables Inn in Foxboro, Sunday at Five o'clock. No RSVP would be necessary.

Chapter 4

Dan took his video selection to the counter. He held it up for Bruce to see. "This O.K.?"

Bruce nodded.

Mr. Cabbot finished with the customer in front of Dan. From the exit she said, "The memorial and pot luck dinner-fund-raiser is on Sunday, Mr. Cabbot. We hope you'll be there."

Mr. Cabbot grunted. He turned to Dan and Bruce. "All the Catholics ever think about is sex."

Dan looked at Bruce who raised his eyebrows. "You Catholic, Mr. Cabbot?" Dan asked.

Cabbot ignored him. "You diddling that school teacher?" He asked Bruce.

Bruce looked at him. "You think I'm gonna answer that?"

Cabbot shrugged. "I'm all for it. You're a Jew. You should be diddling the school teacher."

Bruce and Dan looked at each other. Dan tried to piece it together. "Jews don't get enough sex?"

"Jews are O.K. with sex. They write about it in their book. They ain't afraid of sex. They don't pretend not to do it."

He leaned forward on his elbows. "See the Catholics, they're horny bastards. They're hornier than anybody else cuz they gotta pretend like they don't want it all the time. You make sompin' bad and nasty and everybody gets a boner. If it's Taboo, them Catholic's 'll do it."

"Is that so?" Bruce.

"Yeah, that's so smart ass." Mr. Cabbot rang up their video. "You mark my words; that little girl was killed by a Catholic."

"What IS going on with you and Ms. Sinclair?" Dan asked as they walked home.

Bruce told Dan about the thrift store excursion the day before. And about Megan. Dan confessed that he had mentioned

Bruce's attraction to a "hot school teacher" to Jen. It seems she passed that information on to Meg. Anyway, Dan was of the opinion that Meg's only real beef was that she didn't get to be the one to lose interest first.

Bruce told Dan as much of his conversation with Ella, verbatim, that he could remember and finished with, "She is so cute."

"Sounds like she's . . . on the rebound."

Bruce scowled. "No it doesn't."

Dan was silent.

"I don't give a shit if she just broke up with someone." Bruce continued. "You should hear her talk, Dan. She's glad to be here. She left San Francisco cuz she wanted to be here. I'm here. That guy is three thousand miles away."

Dan smiled. "She's got you, buddy." He held up his little finger. "She's got you right here."

Ella sat up in her bed and looked at the collapsible alarm clock. 6:17. On a Saturday morning and she was awake. Ugh.

As the only person she knew on the whole earth who still defied the use of a cell phone, she needed a telephone. The telephone installation woman had been there the day before, and she was ready to be reconnected to the world outside of central Massachusetts. Ella remembered that Krim Kram opened at eight o'clock and they had that great old-fashioned telephone. This was crazy. Why was she awake and thinking about telephones at six in the morning? And why hadn't she seen hide nor hair of Bruce in three days. (Well, this would be the third.) Maybe he had worked things out with Megan after all. Ella was irritated at the prospect of this. She flounced out of bed and banged around the teakettle and her coffee cup. Why should this bother her? He was a child. A charming, interesting, extremely amusing, child. And she was getting far too attached to this child. Two days. They had spent two afternoons together and she was already accustomed to his company. Ella slapped her hand to her forehead. This wasn't good. This was bad. And it was even worse because he hadn't sought out her attentions in two days.

Ella glanced at her new telephone on the seat beside her.

26

She drove slowly down Summer Street. It was only 8:45 in the morning.

Ella didn't see him sitting on her steps until she got out of her car.

He smiled.

"Bruce." She tried to sound casual.

"Morning, pretty woman."

She sat down next to him. "What's all this?"

"Breakfast. Coffee and donuts." He handed her a cup and opened the box.

She looked inside. "Wow, this is great."

They sat and ate in companionable silence until the box and cups were empty.

Bruce asked, "Was Katie Merchant in one of your classes?"

"No. But her older sister Theresa is." Ella looked at Bruce. "Did you know the Merchants?"

Bruce shook his head. "Not really. Not the parents. I've talked to Katie a few times. In a town this size everyone gets to know the kids, at least a little. This is a small town. This kind of thing is a big deal here."

"I think it must be a big deal anywhere."

"You O.K.?"

"Ohhhh, that's what the breakfast was about. Concern." Ella had assumed Bruce was on her doorstep because she was irresistible to him. "Yeah. I'm fine. Surprised, I guess. Like everyone. You?"

Bruce shrugged. "I hope this isn't an epidemic. We had a big scandal last year. People here can get pretty freaked out by shit like this."

"What was the scandal about?"

"Some little kid hanged himself."

"Why?"

Bruce shrugged again. "No one ever said."

"How old was he?"

"Around 12 I think."

"Rumors?"

"A shit-load. But it died down quick. I didn't know much about it at the time. Although," he paused and thought for a minute, "I do remember seeing his Mom around town a few times after... it.

She was always crying. Red eyes. She had red eyes and looked worn out. They left a couple months later."

"Where'd they go?"

"Beats me."

Ella looked around at the brown and red leaves falling onto the grass. The sun was shining but it was cold. Everything smelled crisp, clean.

"What have you been up to for the last couple of days?" She asked.

"Miss me?"

"Well, sure."

Bruce grinned at her. "I was being hard to get, but I'm done now."

Ella grinned back. "The man has no shame. I like that."

"You up for a game of flag football?"

Ella glanced at his attire. Sweats, T-shirt, sweatshirt, trusty old baseball cap sitting backwards on his head. So that was what he was all dressed up for.

"When?"

Bruce glanced at his watch. "In 27 minutes at the Amherst common."

Ella jumped up. "Just let me pull on some sweats."

Ella let the stream of warm water rush over her head and back. They had gotten to the common after everyone else. There must have been six other young men watching them approach the field together and Ella thought they all knew. Knew what? Dan had pointed his finger at them and said, "this is FLAG football. You two, no tackling." Ella had tried to look innocent and persecuted, but Bruce had simply said, "Maybe."

Ella had a grand old time. They played to 14 points per game. Bruce always threw to her or screened for her or blocked for her. For the third and final game they had ended up on different teams. Ella had been thrown a bomb and caught it. And Bruce, right there behind her, had wrapped his arms around her waist and whispered, "Gotch ya." Ella had jumped out of his arms as if stung by a bee. She looked shocked.

"You O.K.?" Bruce had asked. Ella simply nodded and tried to smile. Then she wondered what the hell was the matter with her.

His embrace had scared her and that was an unnatural reaction for Ella. She enjoyed flirting as much as anyone, and she was comfortable with Bruce, extremely comfortable. He would have made the perfect candidate for her harmless charms. But his touch had startled her. And that in itself suggested emotion. She didn't have time or energy for emotion right now.

Dan and his girlfriend Jen had driven her home because Bruce had had an errand to run. Back in the monster again. Dan was entertaining, Ella thought. He and Bruce had been born in the same hospital, three months apart. They'd been best friends since fifth grade.

She'd said no movie for her tonight when Bruce had asked. How had she rationalized it? Oh yeah, papers to grade. All Bruce had said was O.K.

The shower and Ella's meditations obscured the sound of the phone as it rang repeatedly. Ella hadn't bought an answering machine. Just the phone had been a big step.

It seemed appropriate that it was raining on Sunday for the memorial service. It was being held inside, in the church, but was non-denominational so the whole town could feel comfortable attending. Bruce and Dan had been there with Bruce's mother. Ella didn't notice them until Dan gave her sweater a little tug and nodded toward Bruce. The proceedings had already begun, as Ella was late, so Bruce grabbed her hand and pulled her into their pew, past Dan, next to himself. She smiled at Mrs. Hurowitz who didn't seem to find the whole familiarity the least bit surprising. Mrs. Hurowitz gave a pleasant, little wave and then disregarded them.

Ella watched the activities at the Alter. Candles were being lit and instruments were being tuned. Mrs. Merchant could be heard sobbing. Ella could only see her somberly clad back. She was in black with an old fashioned pill box hat on. Ruth Merchant, mother of the deceased. What was that like? After giving birth and raising some one, a daughter you expected to... that you had expectations of, that should outlive you, that would some day maybe have a daughter of her own. And yet suddenly, one day, ten short years later, she dies. She gets brutally murdered.

Ella's musing was interrupted by Ruth's sudden rush from the church. She pushed past her husband, crying out in anguish, a terrifying noise, and then clutching at her mouth and squeezing her lips together. She stumbled and fell in the aisle with only one hand free to break her fall. She scrambled back to her feet and swerved into the women's rest rooms. Ella pushed past Bruce and ran after her.

When Ella entered the rest room Ruth was leaning over vomiting stomach bile into the garbage can. Ruth's hands were shaking, and she was gasping for air between convulsions. Ella approached her slowly.

"Let me get you some water."

Ruth remained quiet.

Ella grabbed a Dixie cup and filled it with tepid tap water. Ruth took it willingly and swallowed the 3 ounces in one gulp. Then she promptly threw it back up.

Ella leaned against the counter with her hand resting lightly on Ruth's shoulder.

"Do you want to go home?"

Ruth slowly turned her face to Ella.

"God have mercy on you that your baby never gets taken from you."

"Mrs. Merchant..."

But the bathroom door was pushed open and music flooded in with a large matronly woman in a navy blue "sailor" dress before Ella could finish her sentence.

"Ruth, honey, you've got to come back out there."

Ruth's mournful eyes stared at the newcomer. "Yes, I know, Betsy. I'm coming."

Ella slid back in to the pew between Bruce and Dan.

"How'd it go?" Bruce asked.

"Weird." Ella answered. She looked over to where Ruth was standing next to Alwin. Alwin Merchant was stone faced, not touching his wife, still and silent.

Dan was watching the Merchants also.

"What are they like?" She asked him.

Dan crocked his head to the side a little. "They're typical, I guess. She plays the Organ for Sunday Services, he starts drinking right after work, and sometimes they pack up their family and go away for the weekend. She's got family in South Weymouth."

"More concise than I expected, Dan. Thanks."

Bruce had been listening to Dan's image of the Merchants. He leaned forward. "Katie was a nice kid. She used to ask me to fix her bike a lot. Little things were always falling off it."

"And you're good at bikes!" Ella beamed at him just as the musical trio struck up *Amazing Grace*. Everyone fell silent.

After the service Mrs. Hurowitz had invited Ella over for dinner, which she declined. She couldn't miss this meeting with Janice Elderby and risk never finding out why she was screwing Father Dillard. Lydia insisted on a rain check and then set the date for the next Sunday. Ella had thanked her, waved at Dan and Bruce, and made a dash through the rain to her car.

Janice was already seated, looking impeccable, when Ella arrived.

"I suppose you're wondering why I asked you to join me." Janice said after they ordered tea.

Ella fought with her conscience. "Look, Ms. Elderby, what you do is entirely up to you. I didn't tell anyone about it and I don't intend to."

Janice raised an eyebrow. "I want to talk about Jason. I'm worried about him."

Ella doubted that. Still the sudden shift in topic had been a remarkably easy transition for Janice. Ella was impressed.

"Has he always been so shy?" Ella asked.

"Not when he was young. He was precocious. He was always somewhat serious, not an especially playful boy. But now he is so withdrawn."

Ella began to warm toward Janice the mother, if not the woman.

"How long has he been withdrawing?"

Janice hesitated. She didn't know. That was what was worrying her. She didn't know how long Jason had been like this because for a certain length of time now she hadn't been paying any attention. It was only in the last few days when she had noticed that Jason wouldn't look at her or talk to her about school. He wasn't curious about things. There had been a time when Jason asked questions constantly. It had infuriated her at times. Doug had been no help at all. He ignored their oldest son most of the time. Even if he had noticed the change he wouldn't have said anything to Janice. Jason didn't ask questions anymore. It was only two months into the school year, but his grades for the first time ever were mediocre. And he looked so tired. All the time.

Ella thought Janice looked tired.

"What does Jason say?" She asked.

Janice shook her head. "Jason . . . is not an emotional boy. He doesn't talk about things that are bothering him."

I wonder where he gets it? Ella thought.

"Every child is emotional, Ms. Elderby, it's natural. If you think something is bothering him you should find someone he can talk to about it."

There was a silence and Ella wondered if she had offended Janice.

Janice laid a perfectly manicured hand on her spoon and turned it over. "Perhaps he could speak with you?"

"I was thinking more of a therapist, or perhaps a..." Ella stopped.

Janice raised her eyebrows and smirked. "A Priest?"

Ella shrugged. Actually she would never had suggested someone non-secular except that she'd read it in Dear Abby that morning and it had stuck.

Janice leaned back. "For a moment I thought you were quite noble, Ms. Sinclair. 'My business' and all that. Well, young lady, don't bother to judge me. I haven't noticed you with any children of your own or a husband, even a partner, unless that's what you call the Hurowitz boy you seem to be seducing."

Damn, this is an interesting town! Thought Ella.

Janice continued. "I don't think our situations are comparable. Nor are our positions." She paused for effect. "You are new and an outsider, and that is the bottom of the totem pole. Don't threaten me or I'll bite back."

Ella scowled and then shook her head in disbelief.

"Look Ms. Elderby," she laid her napkin on the table, "I don't care who you think you are, this is North Brooktown. Get it? North Brooktown! I'm not in with the gossips. Hell, I don't even know who they are. And I don't really give a crap. And you're right. I don't have children or a husband. But if I did I think I'd think twice about what I could ruin for life before having an affair with my clergyman."

Ella grabbed her bag and coat. She lowered her voice. "Keep in mind, Ms. Elderby, what I witnessed someone else may have already been privy to. The confessional in a public church is not the most discreet place in the whole world."

Bernice leaned back against the couch as Mike drove his tongue deeper into her mouth while his hands fumbled with her blouse.

"I can't get this goddamn thing open." He said as he tried to unhook the clasp to her bra.

Bernice pushed him away. "It's not that tough, honey." She stood up and slipped her shirt off. With meticulous movement she unhooked and removed her bra. Slowly and seductively she massaged her plump, milk-white breasts.

Mike fumbled quickly at his crotch. He unbuttoned his jeans without glancing away from Bernice even for a moment. He masturbated while she striped for him.

From the other side of the window all that was still visible was Mike moving up and down on top of Bernice, clutching at her buttocks with her large white legs wrapped around his waist. It couldn't have been made more sterile for a blockbuster, but Jason watched very carefully.

Ella stared at her stack of 57 collages from two world history classes. If she were just in the mood for it she knew they would be fun and entertaining, and insightful. But she wasn't in the mood for it. She kept thinking about Janice Elderby's threat. Ella knew Janice could stir up trouble if she wanted to. The potential of the Elderbys controlling much of the school board was quite great. But what really got Ella thinking was Janice's comment about Bruce. Seducing? Was that what she was doing?

Ella grabbed her Cubs cap off the mantle and pulled it on, visor to the back. She looked in the mirror. Bruce. He was cute. He made her feel unique. Important. So had Chris. Ella thought about the night she told Chris she had been offered a position in Brooktown, Massachusetts, as a teacher. There had been a long silence until Chris had said, "That's great, hon. If you can get one there, you can get one here." But she had wanted that job. She had explained to Chris how much she wanted to live in Massachusetts, in a small town. She liked it there. If felt like home. Chris had said, "I like it here. This feels like home."

The doorbell rang. Ella jumped.

Chapter 5

Bruce had his hands in his jeans pockets and a warm jacket on.

"Wanna take a walk? It stopped raining."

They ambled slowly down Elm, then turned up Dorsett. Neither one of them spoke. Both of them were pensive.

"Whatch ya thinking about?" Bruce intruded on her self-analysis.

Ella opened her mouth but nothing came out. What could she say? You?

She smiled at the ground.

"Must've been good." Bruce remarked.

"What were you thinking about?"

"I asked you first."

"Ms. Elderby is worried about Jason. She wants me to talk to him. To find out what's troubling him."

"Are you going to?"

Ella looked at Bruce. "I don't really want to. I'm not a therapist. But sometimes I think that's what parents expect."

"That's part of the big 'Learn values in school' debate, isn't it?"

"Well, you're not ignorant at all, are you Mr. Hurowitz?"

"Ms. Sinclair, I'm starting to suspect that you have a condescending attitude toward we small town folk."

"If I did you would certainly set me straight, wouldn't you."

"Anything for my fellow hick."

An amicable silence ensued. Ella stole a glance at Bruce and decided he looked satisfied.

"Bruce, Ms. Elderby threatened me."

"Cuz you don't want to talk to Jason?" Bruce was surprised.

"Well, no, not really. Janice has a secret and I know it. She thought I might squeal I guess."

"Must be a hell of a secret." Bruce didn't seem to care

much.

"It is Bruce. It's a hell of a secret, and I've got to tell someone, and, guess what. You're the only person I trust."

Bruce stopped walking. They had reached the short stone wall to the graveyard.

Ella stopped too and looked questioningly at Bruce.

"You trust me?" He asked.

"Yeah."

Bruce nodded toward the bench across the street. "The bench, or the wall?"

Ella sat down on the wall and pulled her legs up under her. Once Bruce was settled she relayed her encounter with Janice and John Dillard in the church and then told Bruce about her conversation with Janice at tea.

Bruce sat unresponsive for a minute after Ella finished her narration. Finally he said, "I don't think you're the only one who knows Ms. Elderby's secret." He told her about Mr. Cabott's theory on the Catholics and sex.

Ella laughed. "Wow. That's not an uncommon point of view, I've just never heard it put quite so delicately before. You think that means he knows, though?"

Bruce shrugged. "Could."

Ella nodded. "It could."

They were walking back down Summer Street toward Ella's house.

"You never told me what you were thinking about." She nudged him.

"I was thinking about the same thing I'm always thinking about."

"Yeah?" Ella smiled. "What's that?"

Bruce shook his head. He was smiling. "You don't want to open that can of worms, Ella."

"Maybe I do."

"Well, maybe you do, but I think you're too chicken."

Ella unlocked her door. "Too chicken, huh? That sounds like a challenge, Mr. Hurowitz."

"I guess a challenge would be a pretty shrewd move on my part, wouldn't it?" Bruce stood in her doorway.

"That depends. Do you really want to tell me what you

36

think about?"

Ella pushed the door open, motioned for him to enter and raised her eyebrows.

Bruce unzipped his jacket as he stepped inside. He wandered over to the fireplace and leaned against it. Ella glanced up and caught her breath, quickly and quietly. His leaning form was breath-taking and her arms longed to wrap around him.

She approached him. "O.K., go ahead."

"O.K., but there's a condition."

"Yeah? What is it?"

"You have to be honest with me, Ella. Totally honest."

She thought for a moment. It was the caveat she was least inclined to accept normally.

"O.K."

Bruce took a breath and stared at her. "I was thinking about you. I'm always thinking about you. I think about kissing you and holding you and making love to you. And today I was thinking about whether or not you want me to."

There was silence. Bruce looked at her. "C'mon Ella."

"I s'pose I have to answer that." It wasn't a question. She signed. "Bruce…."

Suddenly Ella stopped. She looked surprised. Bruce watched her. A revelation?

"I'll answer your question, Bruce, but you'll have to leave. C'mon." She motioned for him get up. "I'll tell you at the door."

Bruce frowned as he stood up. He grabbed his jacket and walked to the front door.

Ella faced him but didn't look at him. He stood with his hands in his pockets.

"I'd love to be held and kissed and made love to by you. There. Now go."

Bruce moved forward to embrace her. Ella stepped deftly away and backed into the wall.

"Don't touch me, Bruce."

Bruce grinned. "C'mon, Ella. One little kiss. No? How 'bout a hug? Just let me hold you."

Ella shook her finger at him. "Just you stay away from me young man. I don't want to start anything. It's merely a desire, not a possibility. You get the difference, right? I'd like those things. I'm very attracted to you. But there's just no way."

"I knew this was mutual." Bruce was grinning at her.

"Yeah, there's an attraction, but it doesn't have to go anywhere."

"No, 'course not. Why would it? Two available people, as good-looking and witty as we both are, attracted to each other, who like spending time together. Why would something like that go anywhere?"

"Precisely."

"Ella, I'm about to go nuts. At least me hold you for a minute."

"No, no, no, no, no."

Bruce took a hold of her arms and gently pulled her toward himself. She went with out protest. He wrapped his arms around her waist and she buried her face in his shoulder. The embrace felt wonderful to Ella. It had been so long. They were rocking gently and Ella realized she didn't want to let go any more than Bruce wanted to.

Finally she slowly pulled away from him and said, "I think you should go."

He put his hand on the back of her head and kissed her forehead softly.

Ella closed her eyes as his lips lingered on her forehead.

"Goodnight Beautiful."

He let her go and moved quietly out the door closing it behind him.

Janice Elderby set the videotape on the counter.

"I think you should know, Mr. Cabbot, the quality of this tape is atrocious."

Mr. Cabbot leaned onto the counter and grinned at her.

"What do you care about the quality of a tape, little lady? You got better things to do than watch movies, I'm sure."

Janice's look registered disgust. "I don't like your tone."

"Well, that's a darn shame. I guess you think you can be pretty high falutin' around me, but I'd be a little nicer if I was you. You never know, I might just start raisin' the prices." He chuckled.

"I'm leaving, Mr. Cabbot." She said firmly.

"By the way, little lady . . . now hold on, you're gonna

wanna hear this!"

Janice stopped in the entryway and faced him.

"What?" She snapped.

"Your son, Jason, he's been spending an awful lot of time in the porno section, if you know what I mean."

Janice stood completely still. Her son was ten. What was he doing looking for smut videos?

Mr. Cabbot scratched his crotch.

"Seems mighty interested in sex. I guess he's his mother's son, eh?"

"That will be enough, Mr. Cabbot." Janice left the store.

Janice ran up the stairs to her son's room. No one would be home. The kids were at school and Doug was at the University. She would be uninterrupted in her search. Search for what? She prayed there would be nothing to find. No discoveries. Jason was a good boy. He always had been. He was so easy. Never even cried much as a baby. She didn't need to look, she promised herself. After this she would never look again. Janice had promised herself when she had first learned she was pregnant that she would always regard her children's privacy as sovereign. Privacy would foster individuality and trust, she had read. Doug had agreed with her. None of that made any difference at this moment. Her son was making a spectacle of himself in front of a blackmailing son of a bitch like Cabbot. Jason had been so confined lately, so aloof. Perhaps this sexual confusion was behind his odd behavior.

She went through his closet and drawers, but it was under his bed that she found the magazines and tapes. The shock forced Janice onto the floor. She sat and stared incomprehensibly at the graphic, somewhat violent content in the paraphernalia before her. It was her fault. She had failed as a mother. Janice picked up the loot and walked slowly back downstairs to the kitchen.

Ella sat in Stephanie's car.

"So, did you sleep with him?" Stephanie asked.

Stephanie was the only woman Ella had met in the last two months with whom she had felt the least connection. But the connection had been instant and mutual. Stephanie was a few years younger than Ella and also a first year teacher. But Stephanie's life was a picture of stability and satisfaction. It wasn't just the marriage and house that made her seem so stable, it was the complete assurance with which Stephanie approached every endeavor. Like teaching. Ella, on the other hand, Stephanie had once told her, represented all the daring approaches to life Stephanie had no patience for in her own existence.

"Listening to you is like having a vicarious life, that doesn't ever make me hurt."

Ella had laughed and said, "that's only because I don't tell you about all the nights I sit at home and play solitaire."

They were enroute to Stephanie's house for dinner.

"Did you guys make love?" Stephanie demanded.

"No. Of course not!"

"Why? What's so of course about it? He wants you. You want him. You're not getting any. Even if he is, he'll be wearing a condom anyway. You're both adults. You don't have roommates . . ."

"Sex is an entanglement, a complication. Even if you both agree it's not going to be, it is. It always is. And if it's only an entanglement for one party then it's even worse. One person always ends of getting hurt in those situations. Besides, I don't even believe that shit works. This probably sounds horribly cliché and not the least bit chic, but sex is best for me when it involves my emotions. And I don't want to get emotionally involved."

Stephanie pulled up to a red light and turned to Ella. "Girl, you know what I'm gonna say to that!"

Ella shrugged and looked out the window.

Stephanie started driving again. "You already are emotionally involved. And just because you don't fuck him don't mean for one minute that you don't want to fuck him!"

"I'm not denying that I want to fuck him. I'm merely saying I can handle lust, what I don't want to get caught up in is . . . any sort of attachment."

"Well I don't think that would be a problem if you weren't already attached. Dig?"

"Steph . . ."

"No, no, no, Ella. You should hear yourself. You talk about this guy all the time. For the last week you've been happier, cheerful, ever since he helped you with that damn bike! Girl, you are wasting my time trying to deny this!"

Ella shut up. An image of Bruce with his backwards

baseball cap flashed across her mind. Involuntarily she smiled. She wouldn't get to see his sweet face at all today. She would get home too late to see him. Bruce had such a charming smile. So had Chris. There he was again. Was he seeing anyone? Did he have a new girlfriend? Ella's stomach ached. She pushed away the thoughts of Chris with his arm around another woman's shoulder.

Ella looked at Stephanie who was retelling the flag football game almost verbatim as Ella had told it to her. She was mocking Ella's voice and emphasizing the adjectives. Ella chuckled. Stephanie certainly knew how to make her point.

Chapter 6

Ella stopped by Ames on her way home from work to pick up candy. It was Halloween and the trick-or-treaters would certainly be out in full force in N. Brooktown. She was looking forward to it. Many of the kids had shown up for classes in costumes and they'd spent more time discussing what they represented and why they'd chosen that costume than they had on any actual schoolwork. But it had been well worth the diversion.

The doorbell rang. Ella rushed down the hall calling "coming", with a bowl filled with tootsie rolls. She pulled the door open expecting goblins, caterpillars, and cowboys, and found Bruce.

She smiled. "Hey there little boy. What are you supposed to be?"

"I'm the boy next door hoping to take the girl next door out to dinner."

"We can't go out, it's Halloween." Ella pulled him inside. "C'mon help me feed the trick-or-treaters."

Ella started towards the kitchen. She glanced back at Bruce, then looked again. He looked so handsome. He was wearing a sweater and jeans and no baseball cap backwards or otherwise. He was staring at her and it made her catch her breath.

"Do you want to just eat here? I have soup."

"What kind?"

Ella opened the cupboard over the toaster.

"Black bean, Minestrone, and Lentil vegetable."

Bruce stood right behind her. Ella could feel him there. She could smell him and almost touch him. He reached over her shoulder, his arm next to her cheek. Ella stared at the soups.

"Minestrone."

Ella grabbed it from him. "O.K., go get a pot." She was all efficiency. Bruce put the pot on the stove while Ella opened the can.

"Are you nervous Ms. Sinclair?"

Ella smirked. "Why would I be nervous?"

Bruce leaned against the counter. "I thought maybe you

were avoiding me yesterday."

No response.

"Does my being here make you uncomfortable?"

Ella made a big show of rinsing out the soup can and throwing it away.

Bruce waited. "Ella, c'mon. Talk to me."

Ella sighed. "Bruce you're twenty two. I'm twenty nine." She looked at him. "That's seven years."

"You are so pretty."

Ella dropped her head back. "You're not listening to me, Bruce!"

"That's not true." He denied. "I hang on every word you say."

"Bruce..." she hesitated, "Ms. Elderby accused me of seducing you. It made me think. It made me feel guilty."

"Jesus Christ, Ella." Bruce shook his head. "If we were having this conversation and the roles were reversed, if I were twenty nine and you were twenty two, you'd be pissed as hell. You'd think I was a condescending asshole."

"Touché" she mumbled.

"You're standing there telling me to get lost. If this is seduction, you suck at it."

"I'm not telling you to get lost. I don't want that at all."

"Oh yeah, you're just as attracted to me as I am to you." Bruce moved closer to her. "Well I don't think that's true. When we're walking together in the moonlight I'm thinking about you, about touching you. You're thinking about Ms. Elderby's problems with her son."

When she didn't say anything he continued. "The age thing is bullshit, Ella. You know it is."

"I think you're just horny. And now you're disappointed because I'm not going to bed with you."

Dead silence. Bruce stared at her. Ella squirmed. Finally he looked away. He straightened up and reached for his jacket.

"O.K. Ella. I'm gonna leave now before I lose my temper."

"Bruce," Ella was suddenly afraid. What if he gave up? "I wasn't thinking about Ms. Elderby or her problems. I was thinking about you."

Bruce looked at her.

"I was trying to rationalize why it feels so good to me when you're around. And right at that moment you asked me what I was thinking. I didn't want to open that can of worms."

"So what is it, Ella? I can't touch you or even stand near you, because . . . why?"

"I'm just not ready for that yet, Bruce." Ella thumped the counter with her hand.

"You sure felt ready last night." Bruce nodded toward the front door.

"The hug felt wonderful. It did! But I'm not ready to make love. I don't even think I'd be comfortable kissing anyone yet."

"You don't want to make love to me. You don't even want to kiss me. And you call that an attraction?"

Ella ran a hand through her hair and sighed. "I guess that sounds strange. When you put it like that."

"I think it sounds like a heap a' shit. I think you do want to get involved with me but you won't cuz you're hoping if you hold off long enough Mr. San Francisco'll come to town and want you back. And you don't want to have to explain why I'm around if he does."

Bruce waited.

Ella said nothing.

He sat down and put his head in his hands.

"Fuck."

After a minute he stood up. "You could've just told me from the beginning that you were still in love with this guy. I know when to back off."

"Maybe I didn't want you to back off."

"What do you want?"

"I want to have you around. I want to keep feeling as comfortable with you as I have been. I want things to keep feeling just the way they feel right now."

"I feel like shit right now."

"Why, Bruce? Because some woman you've been wanting to screw for the last week has feelings for her ex-boyfriend? Come on! Sex aside, we were developing a really good friendship."

"No. You were developing a really good friendship. I was falling in love."

Ella threw the wooden spoon she was holding onto the counter.

"BULL shit!" She pointed her finger at him. "You have known me for one week. How do you fall in love with someone after one week?"

"I fell in love with you the minute I saw you. That day you asked me for directions, you probably don't even remember it was me, you got out of your car and smiled. And..." Bruce stopped. He looked at her. "Why did you tell me he wasn't ever coming out here?"

"Because Chris isn't ever coming out here."

"Great. Chris. I really wanted to know his name is Chris."

Ella ignored his sarcasm. "Why did you tell me you didn't have a girlfriend?"

"Megan wasn't my girlfriend."

"Oh yeah, that was completely obvious by the way she called you a lying, cheating, whatever."

"Son of a bitch."

"What?"

"A lying, cheating, son of a bitch."

"Thank you."

"And why do you care? How can you be jealous of Meg when you're in love with your ex-boyfriend?"

"I'm not jealous of Megan Barzoff." Ella sounded indignant.

For the first time Bruce started to smile. "Oh yes you are. You even remembered her last name."

"So what?" Ella scowled. "I'm good with names."

"You know what I think?"

Ella shrugged.

"I think even if your little buddy does show up from California there are going to be some problems in paradise."

Ella turned away and started drying off her dishes with a hand towel. Bruce scooted around to her and leaned over onto the counter so he could see her face. Ella refused to look directly at him.

"You know why?" He said as he smoothed a piece of her hair behind her ear.

Ella snapped, "No. And I don't care."

Bruce grinned. "Because, beautiful, you have a mountain of a crush on me and I'm right here. I love you. And I'm not just going to go away."

Ella looked at him. He was right. He was absolutely right.

"You're right, Bruce. I do have a mountain of a crush on you."

Bruce was smiling at her and Ella couldn't help but stare back.

"And I do remember you from the first day I drove into town. I pretty much knew where Summer street was cuz I'd been here before once, but I wasn't quite positive and you just looked so cute sitting there I thought I might as well stop and ask."

He pulled her toward him and put his arms around her.

Ella said, "I thought you were eighteen."

"I thought you were too good to be true."

Just then the doorbell rang.

Bruce let go and Ella ran to answer the door.

"Trick or treat! Trick or treat!"

Bruce heard the calls from the kitchen. He walked into the hall and watched Ella dispense the tootsie rolls. She was so easy to watch. She shut the door and turned around and smiled at him.

"Did you see the flower? She was only a year old. Her Mom made her costume. Her head had a big leaf on the top. She was so cute."

"What were you for your first Halloween?" Bruce asked.

"A pumpkin. What were you?"

"A Bee."

Ella smiled. "I'll have to see a picture of that."

"You bet."

There was a long silence while they stared at each other.

"I'd better go."

Bruce opened the door and stood outside. The night was cold and helped calm him down. Ella stood in the door shivering.

"I'll see you soon?"

Bruce nodded. "Tomorrow."

Ella smiled. "O.K."

Bruce leaned against the doorframe. "I really want to kiss you."

Ella swallowed. "Go away, Bruce. I'm not thinking straight around you."

She shut the door.

Bruce walked home grinning.

Chapter 7

Bruce and Dan sat on the green at Worcester State College. Dan was giggling at the commentary of the DJ on the pocket radio they were listening to.

"I love this guy!" He said to Bruce.

"Huh?"

"Tim Speed?" Dan reminded him.

"Oh yeah, he's good." Bruce wasn't very interested.

"Shit, Bruce. What is wrong with you? It's like you don't have a brain left since this woman moved to town. What's so great about her anyway?"

"She's different. She makes me think."

Dan mumbled something.

"What?"

"I said, she's gotten to your head all right."

Bruce smiled. "Fuck you."

He dropped back onto the grass and stared up at the clouds. "She is pretty hot, though."

Dan scrunched up his face. He didn't agree.

"She's got a nice ass."

Bruce propped himself up on his elbows and looked at Dan caustically. "Yeah? You have to stare at Ella's ass?"

"It's hard to miss."

Bruce had to give him that.

Dan turned the radio down as Tim Speed signed off.

"So you think you finally found one you'll like for more than two months?"

"If she lets me. Danny-boy, I think I'm in love with this one."

"You do?" Dan was frowning. "Why?"

"She's all I think about. And it feels so natural to be around her. To talk to her. I want to be with her all the time. I'd be with her right now if I could be. Every time I think about her I get . . . "

"I see bad things on the horizon for you." Dan interrupted

him. "She's gonna break your heart, buddy."

Bruce stared at the sky. "I know."

"How does she feel about you?"

"I don't know. I know she likes me. But I don't know how much."

"Do you really think something'll come of it?"

"I think I'd stand a better chance if it weren't for Chris."

"Who's Chris?"

"A fucking asshole from what I can tell."

"He's Ella's main squeeze?"

"Not anymore."

"So, who is he?"

Bruce told Dan about Chris.

Dan thought for awhile and then said, "You always fall for women you can't have, Bruce. You got this whole world of uncomplicated babes, right here. With Megan leading the parade." He shook his head. "What the fuck is wrong with you?"

Bruce smiled slowly at him. "You've just never felt the way I feel when I'm around her."

"So I'd jack off a lot. But *I* would stay the fuck away from her!"

"I can't."

"So you gonna play in the game tonight?"

Dan had mentioned to Bruce that they needed a forward. Bruce was a good soccer player and first choice.

"I forgot about it. Sorry, man. I made other plans."

Dan shook his head. "Really? She's better than a soccer game? For *you?*"

"Any date's better than soccer."

"Not for you, dude, it ain't. Not that I've ever noticed before."

Bruce shook his head and smiled. "What, you're gonna lose the game if I don't play?"

"We may lose anyway, dude. These guys are good."

Bruce kept a small grin on his face as he considered the grass. After a contemplative silence he said, "O.K. I'll play."

Dan looked surprised. "What happened to your plans?"

Bruce merely shrugged and flopped back on his back to stare at the sky.

Ella stared out her front room window at the street. The nights were getting colder. The wind made her shutters creak and the chimes go crazy. She sipped her hot chocolate pensively.

Stood-up by Bruce. She had been stood-up by Bruce. She should've known better. Until tonight she thought she hadn't been falling for all his sweet nothings. Now she realized she had. She was a fool.

"Douglas, we need to talk about our son." Janice slapped the magazines and video on the kitchen table in front of his newspaper.

He looked at the Penthouse cover and then looked at his wife.

"What's all this?"

"It's what he's been stashing under his mattress. I found it there after Cabbot informed me that Jason was spending a lot of time in the Adult section."

"Cabbot's an asshole."

Janice grabbed the video and shook it in Doug's face.

"But it's true, Doug!" She snapped. "It doesn't matter if Cabbot's an asshole, our son is watching pornography! Don't you get it?"

"Hey! Don't get short with me! I'm not the one bringing home the trash, O.K.?"

"And I wouldn't really care if you were, Doug." Janice yelled. "But for once we're not talking about you. We're talking about a ten year old boy who is confused."

Doug stood up and stuck his finger out at her. "My whole point is that you wouldn't really care, would you, Jan?"

Janice stopped for a moment. Then she dropped the video back on the table.

"Jesus Christ, Doug. Our ten-year-old boy is making a fool of himself and of us in front of the sleaziest element of town. He just doesn't seem to understand about . . . well, sex OR reputation. This behavior needs to stop."

A silent tension ensued.

Finally Doug said, "O.K. I'll talk to him."

Jason stomped down Porter Street. He had never been so humiliated in his whole life. His father standing there embarrassed and awkward trying to tell him that sex was a beautiful thing between two people who were married. Like him and Mom? Did they have...? Jason didn't want to think about it. Besides all Mom and Dad did when they weren't fighting was ignore each other. Dad never did anything with them anymore. He used to play games with them sometimes. Some of the games were really cool, like when Danielle used sit on Dad's back and then he and Dad would pretend to be dinosaurs and crawl around the living room making growling, bellowing noises. That was fun. It used to be fun. But that was kids stuff anyway and he was getting too old for it. Besides every time he tried to get Dad's attention now he got in trouble for being too loud.

Dad made him feel so stupid as he stood in his room with that stuff in his hands, all red in the face, telling him his "feelings" were normal. Like he would know. He doesn't know anything.

All he does is make me feel stupid. He thinks I'm stupid, Jason thought. He thinks *I* don't know.

Jason wondered how they found his stuff. Brad Petersen must've told somebody he gave Jason that video. Brad liked giving little kids stuff. Nasty stuff. And then he liked telling people about it.

Jason's mind lingered over the thought of the video. He only got to watch it one time. But it was almost burned in his memory. Especially the lady with the blond hairs down there. Pussy. That's what Brad Peterson had told him it was called down there. Thinking about her blond hairs made the ache of fear and self-reproach in his stomach settle into a warm hum of adrenaline.

He was nearing Bernice's house. He walked by her house every night that he could get out. She liked to do it on the couch in her den at the back of the house. And it seemed like the curtains were always open just enough. Jason hoped some day he could marry Bernice.

Father Dillard declined another piece of Mrs. Donnelly's apple-rhubarb pie. This was the first dinner invitation he had accepted from his parish members since arriving in North Brooktown. He didn't especially care for the Donnelly's, but they showed up regularly on Sundays and always deposited into the collection basket and John thought it was necessary to reinforce the habits of this dying breed. Mrs. Donnelly was embarrassingly obvious with her flirtations, but John was a handsome man who knew that his vow of celibacy made him even more attractive. He was not unaccustomed to the attention of certain types of women. He knew how to handle it. He knew he could charm certain people easily. It was an extremely beneficial skill. Mrs. Donnelly was one of those easily charmed women. One of many. John avoided stereotyping, though generalizations were easy to make. He glanced at her daughter Cindy. Now she was . . .

"Father Dillard, will you help me get some more wood from the pile?" Cindy smiled at him.

"Yes, do that John. And then we'll have coffee in front of the fireplace." Mrs. Donnelly said as she cleared plates.

John looked at Mr. Donnelly who grunted and opened the top button of his pants.

Cindy bent over the woodpile very slowly. When she straightened up she said, "I have this paper to write, John. Is it O.K. if I call you John?"

John smiled. "I call you Cindy."

She smiled slowly. "Well, it's about the Scarlet Letter. And I was wondering if I could come to your office and discuss it with you?"

John frowned. He was uncomfortable. "Your teacher should be giving you more guidance. What is our public high school coming to!" He turned to the woodpile and started grabbing pieces.

"I'm in college." Cindy stated.

Father Dillard swung around and looked at her. "How old are you?"

"I'm eighteen." Cindy moved closer to him. "Eighteen. That's the sexiest word in the English language."

John watched her retreat into the house. He had taken enough human sexuality courses at college before he went to the seminary to believe that Janice Elderby was nearing that perfect age to give him the passion he was after. And she fit his prototype. But Janice hadn't been around in almost a week. And by the look of things it would be a long time before he would see her again. That fucking school-teacher. Cindy was eighteen. Not a child. A young woman. Food for thought.

Ella sipped her coffee as she stared at the same page of her novel that she'd been staring at all lunch period. So, who had just been shot? She read it again.

"So? How'd it go last night?" Stephanie slipped in next to her with her sandwich and cookie.

Ella closed her book and grimaced. "It didn't go last night. He stood me up."

"No!"

"Yes."

"Maybe he got hit by a car."

Ella humphed. "He better have."

"He may have a good reason, Ella."

"Yeah. Like he's very young."

Stephanie raised her eyebrows. "It's raining outside. You turn your nose up a little higher, girl, and you gonna drown."

"Well I can't help but feel that this is one of those games you play when you're young and stupid, Steph."

"My husband plays those games with me now! He's a year older than you, Ella. We've been married two years and he still gets jealous and passive aggressive and pouty and grumpy. Sometimes he even gets dramatic. He acts like a damn fool. And I love it. It makes me feel like he cares, like he *feels* things. I may have to pull teeth to get him to admit it, but when he does, hmm, mm, mm!" Steph took a big bite of her sandwich and chomped happily away.

"Well, not showing up for a date after yapping off all that shit about being in love doesn't make me feel the least bit, 'hmm, mm, mm'."

"Maybe he's feeling a little insecure about where he stands with you. I would've dropped Jon like a hot potato if he had told me he had feelings for his old girlfriend."

"Maybe you wouldn't have if he'd admitted having feelings for you too." Ella said.

"He would have had to be pretty convincing."

Ella glanced at her watch. "Shit, I'm late. I've got to go. We'll talk more about this later. Oh, and Steph? Maybe I wasn't very encouraging. But if he's willing to give up that easily; good riddance!"

Steph replied to Ella's retreating figure, "Now look who's playing games!"

Chapter 8

It had been raining steadily all day. Now it looked as if the heavens had simply opened up to let it all come out.

Ella pulled her car up in front of her house. The puddle between her driveway and front door was too big to negotiate. This would be easier for now.

She sat in her car looking at the rain pelting down on her windshield. Get out and go inside, she told herself.

She stepped out of her car and into the rain, grabbing quickly for her bag of books and papers.

"Ella!"

She turned and saw Bruce jogging over to her. He had his baseball cap on the right way around. Maybe to protect his face from the rain.

Ella faked a little smile and hurried up her stairs. Bruce caught up to her and grabbed her arm.

"Hey."

She glanced at him as she fumbled for her keys.

"Hi Bruce."

"You're pissed."

"Well, yes I am." She opened her door. "But I'll get over it. Bye Bruce."

"Shit. Ella . . ."

She shut the door on him.

Bruce knocked on her door. "C'mon Ella." He yelled through the door. "I want to apologize. Let me talk to you."

"Apology accepted, Bruce. Now go home." Ella yelled back as she retreated to the kitchen and turned on the kettle.

Bruce walked around to the back of the house and knocked on the kitchen door.

"Ella, you gotta talk to me."

"It's raining cats and dogs. Go home!"

Bruce put his hands on his hips and dropped his head back.

54

"I knew this was going to be a fucking struggle." He mumbled to himself. He took a deep breath.

"It's about six o'clock, Ella. Everyone should be getting back from work around now. Maybe I'll just stand out here in the rain and tell you, nice and loud, what I need to tell you."

Ella glanced out the window and he gave her a raised eyebrow.

"Go home, Bruce." She yelled.

She sternly stuffed a tea bag into her mug and poured in the water. She glanced at Bruce through the kitchen door as she went to the front room.

Then next thing Ella heard came from outside the front door.

"IT'S LIKE THIS ELLA. I WAS TALKING TO DAN . . . "
From the first word resonating around the neighborhood to the moment when Ella yanked the door open and hauled Bruce inside, mere seconds passed. Instinct; reaction took over. Yet in those mere seconds her thought raced. What amazing determination this young lover possessed. Not only was his voice frighteningly loud and clear, he was going to say it all, whatever it was, right out there in the open for everyone in this small, gossipy town to hear. The man had no shame. It was a decidedly appealing quality. And he was doing it for her.

She stared at him. "Look at you. You're sopping wet. Go home and dry off. We'll talk later."

"No. You're not getting rid of me."

Ella pushed the door shut. She looked at Bruce with his red cap and sweet face. Warm eyes. Warm smile.

"Well, hang on then." She ran upstairs to her room. "Here. Take off your wet stuff and put that on." She threw the sweat pants and shirt at him and pointed to the bathroom.

He walked into the kitchen and watched Ella putting away her dishes.

"Who's clothes am I wearing?"

Ella looked up at his sweats clad countenance. "What?"

"These aren't yours. Unless you like to buy your clothes from the men's section."

"What does it matter who they belonged to, Mr. Hurowitz.

They're dry."

"I'm going to stand here in the buff unless you tell me didn't belong to Chris."

Ella rolled her eyes at him. "They weren't Chris'. You want some coffee?" She asked.

He shook his head. He threw his clothes in her dryer. "Ella, I'm sorry about last night."

"What the hell happened to you?"

"I just...I couldn't make it."

"Your phone doesn't dial out?"

"Not unless I pick it up and punch the number in."

"So you didn't even try to call me?"

Bruce hesitated. Then, "No."

"So this was no accident, I take it. You changed your mind and didn't bother to tell me. And that's fine. I'm not gonna die because we don't spend an evening together, Bruce. It's just time, company, someone I enjoy talking to. I don't want you to feel like you're required to spend time with me, but make up your god-damn mind and then tell me."

"It wasn't quite that cut and dry, El. I wanted to see you. A whole lot. But then I decided to do something else."

"What?"

"Soccer."

"You were playing a soccer game last night?" Ella snapped.

Bruce sighed. "Yeah. And I want you to let me explain it to you."

Ella pulled out a chair and sat down. "By all means."

Bruce sat on the counter. "I was talking to Dan about us. About how I feel about you. And about how I think you feel about me. Even if you don't want to admit it. And then fucking Chris came up."

Ella scowled. "You told Dan about Chris?"

"My best friend, Ella."

"Fine."

Bruce continued. "And when I told him about it I felt stupid. Like you were using me. Like you wanted it both ways. Me here, for now, and Chris there, maybe for later."

"Who pursued whom here, Bruce!"

"I know that's your rationale, El. But that's bullshit. I

wanted to be with you the minute I saw you, that's true. And I was gonna try no matter what. But you never made me feel like I should stop. You kept giving me just enough encouragement. You know, Ella? Just enough so that later, in retrospect, it looks like I went after you. But at the time . . ." he shook his finger at Ella.

"At the time, what, Bruce?"

"At the time you were responding Ella. Give me a little credit. I know when some one is interested in me. You didn't want me to stop pursuing you."

"Nice job on passing the buck, Bruce." Ella stood up and walked over to the opposite counter. "So you didn't show up last night, or call, after saying you'd be here because you felt like I enticed you into falling in love with me. You had to blow off our date to play soccer with the boys to regain your grasp? What a crock of macho crap!"

Bruce jumped down and moved over to her. "O.K., I was an asshole last night. The more I thought about Chris and you, the more it pissed me off. I feel like that guy is the only thing I can't do anything about. I know you're gonna make it tough for us, Ella. But I can handle that. I *want* to handle that. But Chris... he's like this unknown... thing, that may or may not be a part of our relationship."

"Maybe it's best if our relationship, under the circumstances, stays platonic."

Bruce shook his head. "I knew you'd say something like that. Any chance you get. No way, Ella. I'm not giving up. And I don't think you want me to."

They stared at each other.

He was right. She didn't want him to. She knew she *should* want him to stop persuing her. Intellectually she knew this. But her other voice was whispering it's approval of him, of his beautiful lithe form, his warm blue eyes, his golden crop of hair and his sweet, seductive smile. Ella's gaze shifted between Bruce's lips and his eyes. Both so desirable.

He was watching her watch him. There was no movement besides the clear motion of their slightly burdened breathing. They stood slightly transfixed. Then Bruce leaned in slowly and put his hand in her hair. Ella responded to the gentle pressure guiding her mouth toward his. Her heart began to race. Suddenly the doorbell chimed. Loud and infinitely obnoxious. They broke apart and Bruce muttered "Shit."

"Hey kids. It's stopped raining. We're gathering for a game of multimate. In or out?" Dan tossed his Frisbee to Bruce.

"Multimate?" Ella asked.

"Mud ultimate." Bruce explained.

"Oh. Well then, we're in." Ella answered.

Ella found that it was pretty much the same group of athletes from their football game except Dan's girlfriend Jen was there making it two women amongst the men.

The game was staged in an arena of mud. They confessed that they weren't doing the field any good playing on it right after a big storm, but the lights were on and it was irresistible. It was a county park anyway, so they had every right to be there. Ella had no desire to argue the moral delinquency of ruining the field for everyone else's use. She wanted to play too.

Throwing a wet and muddy Frisbee proved to be a challenge, but it wasn't nearly as difficult as trying to run. Feet were getting stuck, shoes were flying off, slipping, sliding, falling. By the time the game ended Ella was the only one who was clean and dry from the knees up. Bruce pointed it out to her saying there was something wrong with that picture.

Ella shrugged.

Bruce stretched his arms out to her. "Let's have a big hug, beautiful."

"No. No chance in hell. You're caked with mud from head to foot. Go away!"

Bruce started toward her, lips puckered, arms out. "C'mon, baby."

Ella was backing away. "No, Bruce. Don't touch me!"

Bruce lunged forward as Ella's foot sank deep into the mud. His arms were around her in an instant. He held her tightly to him for a second.

Ella smiled. "I guess we're even now."

Bruce scooped a little mud off his shirt and wiped it on her cheek.

"Yeah. Just a little right there, then we're all even."

Then Ella grabbed his shirt pulled him toward her and

kissed him. There was a second of hesitation borne of surprise before Bruce's hand slipped into Ella's hair and around to the back of her head. He pressed her against him, pushing her lips harder against his own. She felt his tongue in her mouth, slow but demanding.

Ella's hormones surged. She could hardly breathe. She pushed Bruce away. She'd been waiting for that kiss for a hundred years. It was everything she had hoped it would be except that it was on a field of mud with a dozen people watching.

Dan yelled. "Lets go, you guys."

Ella and Bruce came back to reality.

Bruce smiled. "Shower time."

"Yes indeed."

Ella thought hers might need to be cold.

Chapter 9

"I'm telling you Chief, I didn't see a thing. I didn't walk Parker in the woods that day because Doc said keep him away from the ticks for a week. I just started takin' him through the woods again this morning."

Galvin Zipher stood in his door scratching Parker on the head.

Chief Morris looked around. "Let's go inside."

Galvin poured out a cup of coffee for the chief.

"Look Vin, I need something. Boston is sending out two detectives to mess in my shit, an' I gotta have somethin' for 'um when they get here."

Galvin looked helpless.

"You didn't see anybody? In the area? Later?"

Galvin shook his head. "But I been thinking. Why would anyone kill that little girl? If we got some sick-o out there raping little kids an' then killin' 'um then maybe we want some help from Boston."

"We ain't looking for some sick-o. Whoever killed that kid knew her."

"Well now how the hell do you know somethin' like that, Chief?"

"No struggle, Vin. No struggle at all. She went there with the person who strangled her. And I think she was already playing touchy feely, an' it just went too far."

Galvin nodded slowly.

Then he asked, "Were we gettin' into sex when we were that young, Chief?"

"I wasn't. But it wasn't for lack of tryin'."

"Maybe these kids need to spend more time reading the words of the good Lord."

The chief shrugged. "I'm sure there's many agree with you, Vin." He patted Parker and left.

Mr. Cabbot watched Dan reading the jackets of several Woody Allen comedies.

Dan set 'Stardust Memories' on the counter.

Mr. Cabbot sneered at his selection. "Trying to impress the school-teacher, son?"

"You're thinking of Bruce, Mr. Cabbot. And I ain't your son."

Cabbot took offense to Dan's tone and growled, "You tell your friend, the Jew, he'd better keep his eyes open. I seen his Missy going to the church. For a little extracurricular activity."

Dan took a moment to let it register.

Then he smiled slowly and said, "What? You think she's fucking the priest?"

"She wouldn't be the first. And she won't be the last."

Dan raised his eyebrows. "You seriously think Ella Sinclair is getting it on with Father Dillard?"

"I think this is the most ignorant town in the USA. If you all weren't such a bunch a' hicks, you might be noticing this shit for yourselves. Well, let me tell you this, smart ass, that school-teacher ain't no hick. She's seen what's going on, an' she's gettin' some of it for herself! I bet she's a catholic too."

"Who all's gettin' it from Dillard?" Dan was now as curious as he was amused.

"Figure it out for yourself, dough boy." Cabbot snarled.

Dan grinned. "Well I'll be sure and pass along your advise to Bruce. Mighty thoughtful of you, Cabbot."

"Go ta hell." Cabbot muttered. "This town'll let any fucking clergyman have it all as long as he don't make no scandal. All they care about is how it looks. You know why Paulie Turtino hanged himself?"

Dan stopped in the doorway. "No. Do you?"

"I got a theory."

Dan waited.

"Let's hear it."

"Ask the school-teacher."

"How the hell would she know? She just got here."

"You tell her to think about it. She'll figure it out."

"You don't have a fucking theory, Cabbot." Dan goaded.

Cabbot grunted. "That shit don't work on me, kid. I been

around a lot longer than you and your friends. Now get the hell out of my store."

      Ella pulled into her driveway. She had gotten home earlier than usual. It was still light outside. With the days getting shorter and shorter it was nice to be home before the sun set.

      She leafed through her mail. Nothing from Chris. Of course she didn't have anything from Chris, he didn't even know her address. He knew she was in North Brooktown, but he couldn't know she was living in the old Eustead place. Despite that she had hoped that somehow he would make the effort to find out. She had distinctly told him when she left not to write or phone her; she would contact him when she was ready. But she had hoped all along that he would disregard that instruction and pursue her with vehemence. Prove to her that she mattered enough to him to find her despite what she said. Ugh! Ella scowled. That was ridiculous! She sounded like the helpless damsel of a trashy romance novel. She was perfectly capable of knowing and choosing what she wanted. Chris was the past. Chris was the past!

      She glanced twice at the hand-lettered envelope of thick ivory paper. It looked like a wedding invitation. Ella tore it open. From the Elderbys. Please attend their "Brooktown Founded Day" party. It was on Monday. Monday. Ella realized that the proximity of the date meant that Janice had not intended initially to invite her at all. She had obviously been a last minute decision. It offered her the option of bringing a guest. Ella grinned.

      Bruce knocked on Ella's door. No response. He walked around to the side of the house. No car in the driveway. Damn. He had to leave in a few minutes and wanted to see her before he left. A whole day and a whole night without even laying eyes on her was an eternity. Would she care? Would she miss him? Would she be thinking about him while he was gone?

      Bruce ran home and scribbled down a note. He wanted to write more. He wanted to write it all. He wanted to talk to her. To look at her. To hold her. Hold her and hold her and hold her. They hadn't said much to each other the night before. Dan had driven them home. Ella had jumped out first, said thanks, smiled at Bruce and said, "I'll see you tomorrow", and then rushed inside. He had wanted to kiss her. Hell, she had kissed *him*! She'd taken that step. The step had been taken. Now he was afraid she was going to take it away again. He had to keep the momentum going. Any lull might jeopardize his chances. Where the hell was she? What could he say on a note that would make her understand? That would seduce her? That would make her miss him?

Bruce licked the envelope and sealed it tightly. He shoved it under the heavy brass knocker. He lingered for a moment, looking at the note. Then he turned and walked home.

Father Dillard watched the kids choir practice. It really did sound charming when young voices sang "Prepare Ye." It was one of the few songs that actually moved him. It always had.

Ruth Merchant was a talented music instructor. So unfortunate that this was the only outlet her rather tyrannical husband allowed. Perhaps, for the church at least, it was a blessing in disguise. She had taught the children well. They were now actually grasping the essence of the canticle. By Christmas it would sound wonderful.

Dillard looked around for Jason Elderby. Late again. This was the third week in a row. He heard the wind whistle through the door and saw Jason entering the church. He was dressed in black again. Where did he get these clothes? Dillard would have imagined that Janice Elderby dressed her children more stylishly than that. Preppy was more her style. And with a woman like that, her style was their style. Still it seemed Jason had forged an identity of his own, morbid as it might be.

John considered his role in Jason's delinquency. Yes, he should confront him, he decided.

As Jason walked past Dillard toward the choir, John reached for him.

Jason, as suddenly as a startled vulture, leaped to the side out of John's reach.

"Sorry to scare you, Jason." John was surprised.

Jason looked terrified. "What?"

"I was just wondering why you've been late for practice so much?"

"I don't even want to do this stupid singing stuff!" He was almost yelling.

"O.K., Jason. It's up to..."
Jason ran out of the church without waiting for John to finish.

He walked slowly back toward Bernice's house. It was the only way he felt satisfied anymore. It made his anger go away. Afterwards the guilt was overwhelming, but it always dissipated. And then he had no control. He couldn't stop. And he couldn't tell anyone. Jason had a friend he could talk to once. They used to talk about stuff, all kinds of stuff. Then Brad's Dad got laid off and they moved to Michigan. But it didn't really matter because he probably couldn't tell even Brad this. Brad wouldn't understand. No one would ever understand. This had to stay a secret.

Ella pulled the envelope from its brass prison. It looked like Bruce's semi-legible scrawl. Her heart palpated as she tore it open. "Hey Beautiful," it read. Yep, it was from Bruce. A big smile spread across her face and she crushed the letter against her chest for a second. She went inside before reading the rest.

"I'm sorry I missed you. We're going to Providence tonight for a game in the morning, so I won't get to see you. I guess the kiss last night was for the road. It'll last me. Be good." He had drawn a little heart at the end with his name behind it. Bruce.

Without giving it a second thought Ella raised the letter to her lips and gave it a pensive, loving, kiss.

Chapter 10

Sunday morning the rains finally stopped. The sun returned but the weather had permanently changed. It was markedly colder and the wind was gusty and bitter. The leaves, though still colorful, were getting browner and falling in droves to the ground.

Ella found it invigorating. She took a brisk walk in the morning and thought about how much she would love to have a dog again. Her feet crunched on the brown and red and yellow leaves as she walked. It was a soothing and familiar cadence, one she and her dog had experienced many times together in the past. It had been a few years since her dog and favorite companion of her youth had died. Perhaps now she had settled down enough to take on the responsibility of having a dog again.

How nice it would be to run all this by Bruce, she thought.

Ella unlocked her front door.

"Ella!"

The shout came from behind her. She swung around and saw Bruce and Dan moving quickly toward her. She waved. "How'd the game go?"

Bruce grinned at her. Ella matched his gaze for a second before looking away.

"We won. But listen to this, beautiful, Dan's got a story for you!"

They went inside.

"So what is it?" Ella asked as they sat around her kitchen table.

"I had a little talk with Mr. Cabbot on Friday. He thinks you're screwing the town moral conscience."

Ella frowned. "Huh?"

"He told me to tell Bruce to keep an eye on you, cuz you were visiting the priest."

Ella was getting impatient. "What?"

"Jesus, Dan. Tell her the whole story."

Dan took a breath and began. By the time he had finished Ella had been indignant, disgusted and amused. "Well, what the fuck is he talking about me being able to figure it out?" She asked.

Dan shrugged. "But he seemed pretty certain that you'd know his theory."

"Or maybe that you'd have some theory of your own that's the same as his." Bruce added.

"Well I don't have a theory. I hardly know anything about it except what you told me, Bruce."

"Well maybe the three of us can come up with a plausible theory." Dan suggested.

"O.K. What do you guys think? You were here; why did Paulie hang himself?" Ella put it to them.

"Well, he was a kid at a tough age." Bruce ventured. "Life can pretty much suck when you're twelve."

"That's a given." Ella scribbled it down on a piece of paper. "What did people say about it at the time? There must have been rumors."

"No. That's the weird part. I mean, there were rumors but they were squelched real quick. And then nobody really talked about it." Dan said.

"First they said it was an accident, but everybody knew that was bullshit. No one called 'um on it, so then after awhile they just didn't say anything at all."

"What are the Turtinos like?"

Bruce shrugged. "Don't know them."

Dan cut in. "They're the church-going, up-standing, middle class types."

"Catholic?"

"Catholic."

Ella thought for a moment. "Do you think Mr. Cabbot would have a theory about this if the Turtinos were Protestant?"

Bruce and Dan smiled. "Probably not."

There was a short period of silence where all three of them seemed lost in thought.

Then Ella said, "You know, I was just thinking, why would a twelve year old kill himself? Teenagers kill themselves when they don't see any other way out. You know what I mean? Paulie must have been desperate. He must've thought that whatever was

66

tormenting him, there was no way out and there never would be."

"Yeah, but when you're a kid," Dan suggested, "anything can make you feel like that."

"I didn't feel that way." Ella said. "I mean I felt desperate at times, but only once did I feel like committing suicide. And that was by far the roughest year of my life."

She thought for a moment. "And even then, I think I knew I had options. I mean I must've, because I didn't." She glanced at them. "What about you?"

"I thought about it once." Bruce admitted. "When I lost my soccer scholarship at Amherst College."

Dan shook his head. "I never thought about it. Too many women in the world to leave it any earlier than you have to. By choice, that is."

Ella smiled. "Of course." She tapped her pencil on the pad of paper in front of her. "Well, now that we've all bonded, let's get back to the issue at hand. Why did Paulie hang himself?"

"Or, what reason does Cabbot think Paulie had for hanging himself?"

"Right."

They thought silently for a few minutes.

"What was Paulie like?" Ella asked them both.

"I only saw him around sometimes. I never talked to him or his parents." That was Bruce's contribution.

"What about you, Dan?"

"He struggled a lot. He was a kid who was always struggling. Trying to be liked and trying to get attention. He was loud a lot, but you could tell that he was never sure of anything. I kinda liked the kid, but I didn't want to be around him for long, cuz he was a lot of work. And his Mom was always apologizing for him like he was a dirty spot on her carpet or something. She expected a lot from him. He was the oldest. And he was never gonna measure up."

"Wow, Dan. You sure have that one all figured out."

"No, actually I never thought about it before. It just came to me right now. I guess you just asked the right question, El."

He got up. "Well, kids, it's been enlightening, but I'm hungry. And I'm gonna be late. I've gotta pick Jen up from the crafts fair at 2:00. Shit."

He was mumbling to himself as he grabbed his jacket and rushed down the hall. "Later Bruce. Bye Ella."

"Hey, you coming over for dinner?" Bruce yelled.

"Don't know." He yelled back just before the door slammed shut.

Bruce turned to Ella. "But you are, right?"

Ella had forgotten Lydia's invitation until Bruce mentioned it. "Oh. Yeah."

Bruce got up and put his jacket on.

"You don't have to leave." Ella said.

"I don't want to leave. But I've got to study for a mid-term."

Ella walked him to the door. "Thanks for the sweet note."

She slipped her arms around his waist and hugged him. Bruce put his cheek against her hair and breathed deeply.

He breathed, "soft hair."

Ella looked up at him. Bruce kissed her softly. Ella closed her eyes and waited for more. Bruce caressed her cheek with his finger. He kissed the cheek he had been touching and said, "I've got to go, El."

Ella opened her eyes. "Right this second?"

Bruce nodded. "Yeah. Otherwise . . ."

Ella kissed him.

Bruce moaned. All the desire in him was awake. His arms tightened around her. She was pulled as close to him as possible. Ella's tongue flitted gently over Bruce's as his lunged deeper into her mouth. Ella could hear Bruce's heavy breathing. It almost matched her own. She could feel his warm breath on her cheek. She pushed against him and felt the erection in his jeans. He moaned again and pulled her hips against his, holding her there. In one move Ella was up against the wall. She slipped her hands in Bruce's back pockets. Bruce felt the pressure of Ella's hands, holding him against her. He made minute movements back and forth so she could feel the scope of his erection and he could rub it against her.

Suddenly Ella pushed him away.

"Bruce" she said between breaths, "we'd better stop."

Bruce had stepped back and was leaning over with his hands on his thighs.

Finally he said, "Yeah. Sure."

"Are you O.K.?"

"Right. Just... Fine."

He straightened up, opened the door and stepped outside. The cold air hit him with a blast. It helped. He turned to Ella who stood in the door. "Ella Sinclair, you are a tease!"

"I could say the same."

Bruce smiled and shook his head.

"No you couldn't. I'm not the one stopping us. I'll never be the one stopping us."

"What time should I come over?" Ella changed the subject.

"Six-ish." Bruce was already down the stairs.

He returned Ella's wave half-heartedly.

Ella shut the door and smiled. Bruce was pouting.

Lydia watched her son. She had always lived her own life, Bruce had always lived his. Even when he was very young there had not been much "raising" necessary. Bruce had more or less always been responsible for himself. Lydia had learned to trust that Bruce could take care of himself, completely. She'd never really worried about him. Lydia wasn't a worrier by nature, but even the most relaxed often got gray hair over their children. But Bruce had rarely worried her. She felt that rare, anxious discomfort now. Seeing him in love wasn't the problem. It was Ella. Lydia liked Ella. And she could see where Bruce's infatuation lay. But she didn't trust Ella. Ella liked Bruce. That much was obvious. But there was something distinctly unsettling about Ella Sinclair. Lydia couldn't put her finger on it. Perhaps it was that Ella seemed so certain of herself. She didn't seem to need Bruce. But he thought she did. And she made him believe that she did. Lydia thought that Ella played her cards very carefully, and very well. It would have been easy to despise Ella if it weren't for Ella herself. Lydia and Ella were simpatico.

"This is delicious." Ella interrupted Lydia's thoughts.

Bruce and Greg, Lydia's boyfriend, agreed. Lydia beamed.

After dinner Ella and Bruce took a walk. The night was crisp and clear. The sky was littered with stars.

Ella breathed in deeply.

"It smells so good out here."

"You know Ella, I was thinking. About Cabbot's theory. I

was trying to remember the context of it. Didn't Dan say that Cabbot was in the middle of complaining about the Catholics when he mentioned Paulie's suicide?"

"Yeah. I think so."

"We all agreed Cabbot wouldn't have a theory if it didn't some how tie into Catholicism."

"Indeed."

Ella thought for a moment. This was redundant. Maybe it was the wine that was fogging up their ability to establish innovative analysis on the Paulie Turtino suicide. She knew Bruce was trying to make a point and she knew she should know what it was but she wasn't formulating a clear picture.

"Maybe we should be putting more emphasis on that."

"That's a very astute observation, Mr. Hurowitz. Cabbot must think Paulie's suicide had something to do with him being a catholic. Or maybe Paulie saw Dillard having sex with his mother and he didn't know how to deal with that."

"Dillard came after Paulie killed himself."

"Well what happened to the priest who was here before Dillard?"

Bruce shrugged. "How would I know?"

"You live here, Bruce. I thought maybe the local gossip was unavoidable. Small town stuff."

"You can live in a small town, Ella, without *living* in the small town."

"You've lived here all your life, Bruce. I thought for sure you would *live* here."

"So I guess that's why you feel you can play games with me, huh?"

Ella stopped. "What?"

"Games. That's what you're doing."

"I am not!"

"Yes you are."

Ella scowled. "What are you talking about?"

"Do you want to sleep with me?" Bruce asked her.

Ella looked at him. "I think you know the answer to that."

"What is the answer, Ella. Tell me."

"Yes. I do. But..." Ella held up her fore finger. "I won't."

Bruce snorted. "You want to, but you won't. Why don't you

just say no, Ella?"

"Because you asked me if I *wanted*to, not, if I *will*."

"That's a game."

"Why is it that when sex is involved I'm playing games? What about the games you play?"

"Like what?"

"Like the guilt trip about Chris. Or the pressure to go to bed with you."

"Pressure? What pressure?" Bruce spread his arms out incredulously.

"What do you call this? What's this whole discussion about?"

"This is about you treating me the same way you would treat Chris if I were him."

Ella glared at him. "That is ludicrous!" She yanked her arm away when Bruce reached for her. "I'm going home, Bruce. Tell your Mom thanks."

"Ella, there are women I can fuck. If that's what this were about I wouldn't need come to you."

Ella swung around. "Then what the hell is this about, Bruce? What do you want from me?"

They stood in the middle of the street.   "I want you to give this a chance."

"Goodnight Bruce." Ella strode across the street.

"How did I piss you off this time, Ella?"

"I don't want to hear that shit anymore. I've heard it before." She tried to shut the door but Bruce pushed it open and followed her inside.

"You haven't heard it from me."

"Yeah, I've heard that one too."

"Ella, you're blowing me off cuz of what some one else did. I'm not Chris."

"I don't really want to have this conversation with you, Bruce."

"Well, we're having this conversation. It's happening right now. We're gonna talk about this, Ella."

"Why is this so important to you, Bruce?"

"Because you're so important to me. And because you're assuming that I'm going to be just like Chris. Whatever Chris told you, however he hurt you, that's not me, Ella. I'm not responsible for that. I know how I feel about you. I know I've never felt this way about anyone..."

"Stop, Bruce! Just stop right there!" Ella held up a hand. "Please."

"Jesus fucking Christ, Ella, I'm not Chris!"

"Well, you might as well be. You're saying all the same things. Trying to convince me to trust you in exactly the same manner. It's very charming and you're just as good at it as he was. But I'm not having any. I like you. I like having you around. I want to have you around. But I'm not making any commitments and I don't want you to."

Bruce stared at her. "There's no way I'm gonna get through to you, is there?"

"No."

"Fuck, Ella!"

"You're twenty-two, Bruce. Of course you think this is about love, but it's really about sex. And if I could simply have sex with you I would. But that won't work for me right now."

"You're saying one thing but you don't behave that way, El. You're a hypocrite. You *want* me to be in love with you. You want me to be all over you. You don't treat this friendship any more platonically than I do. The way you look at me. The way you touch me. You think I'm a child? Is that the easiest excuse? That's bullshit. If you're so willing to be friends then treat me like a fucking friend, Ella. Treat me like you treat everybody else."

Ella smiled slowly. "I can't."

"You can't? You *can't?*"

Ella shook her head. "In many ways you're right, Bruce. I do want the attraction to be there. But I'm not willing to let myself go. I can't."

Ella moved over to Bruce. She took his hands in hers. He interlocked his fingers with hers.

"For the sake of this friendship, which I badly need right now, let's stay friends." Ella looked at him. "Please."

Bruce sighed. "It's all up to you."

He paused and they watched each other. "I can't be anything more than you want me to be. But I think you're going to regret letting me go."

"Maybe. Lose the lover, keep the friend."

"I think I can be both."

"Yeah you think that now."

"I'll think that in three years. I'll think that in ten years."

"No you won't. You won't even think that in three months."

"And that's a fact?" Bruce's tone was sharp.

Ella nodded.

"Because that's what happened with Chris?"

"Because that's the way it works, Bruce! And I'm not talking about sex."

"No shit, Ella. I know what you're afraid of."

"You do?"

"What if this works, Ella? What if you and I still want each other in three years? Or in ten years?"

Ella yanked her hands away from Bruce's and scowled. "Oh so what, Bruce! People stay together for 50 years for all sorts of reasons. Never any good ones, mind you."

"No. I said, what if we still *want* each other. What if we're still in love?"

"People don't stay in love."

"What if they do?"

"Oh c'mon, Bruce. Do you really believe that?"

Bruce shrugged. "I don't know Ella. Up until a month ago I would never even have considered it. But now, I don't know. I'm not so sure that I couldn't be in love with you forever."

Ella's heart beat rapidly. He sounded as convincing as Chris had some year and a half ago. But that sentiment was believable to a twenty-two year old.

"Then give me some time. Be my friend."

There was a long silence. Ella watched Bruce. Bruce stared at his hands.

"O.K. Some time." Bruce finally said. "But I don't think you're going to like having me as just your friend."

Ella smiled. "I'm optimistic."

"About some things." Bruce said.

He kissed her softly on the cheek before he left.

No more walking on the clouds, butterflies in the stomach, smiles in an empty room. Nothing to anticipate, no one to look forward to seeing. The day seemed to drag, the kids seemed ordinary, the potted plants seemed to droop. Even worse, Steph was home sick today. No one to talk to about her feelings. Ella sighed. It was lunchtime but she had no appetite. She fished around in her bag for a Kleenex and her hand scraped a sturdy envelope. The invitation! She had completely forgotten. That was tonight.

Ella made steps to the front office and dialed Bruce's number. All the old familiar sensations kicked in. Of course he wouldn't be home. But she'd leave a message.

Chapter 11

Doug watched his wife's elegant form float from cluster to cluster as only the most capable and talented hostesses could manage. She was a perfect partner for the socially inclined. She was incredibly handsome, charming, bright, knowledgeable, and discreet. Behind her Doug spied Danielle's small figure, his sweet little flower-in-her-hair daughter, smiling at one of the guests as she displayed her favorite stuffed animal for inspection. That was his daughter, his and Janice's. They had done a better job as parents with their second than with their first. It was evident in the child herself. Danielle, even at 5 years old had pretty manners, and a sunny disposition. She would make an excellent public figure. She would cultivate Janice's charm and ease with the "right" people. She would be another Janice; beautiful, competent, and dead certain of herself. Little Danielle, cute as a button. Daddy's little girl. Did all second children turn out to be so much easier to take than the first? What was the matter with Jas these days? He was so quiet, so boring. He didn't want to spend any time with the family. He'd changed a lot lately. Just stayed in his room. There'd been a time when he was vivacious and demanding. He'd always been a difficult boy, trying so hard to get attention, and never saying the right thing. But at least he used to try. It seemed like a long time ago now.

Doug tried to remember the days when he thought he was the luckiest man alive. Those were the days when he and Janice had wanted the same things. Back then before the children, and the house, and the obligations. Back then he had wanted so much to have the life he led now. He looked around. This was his dream come true. He stifled a shudder. He glanced around the room gazing at all the attractive, well-dressed young women. So many beautiful women. He watched one flaxen haired beauty in particular as she engaged in animated conversation with two other women. Her breasts were small, barely noticeable, but her ass was well rounded and firm. Despite her attractive derriere it was the hint of the strap of her slip showing at the shoulder of her dress, which first caught Doug's attention. Six or seven images of he and she together flashed through Doug's mind before he closed his eyes and took a long drought from his bourbon on the rocks.

"Are you O.K. Mr. Elderby?"

Doug swung around. It was the school-teacher. Jason's teacher.

He smiled. "I'm fine. Nice to see you, Ms. Sinclair."

"Mmm. Likewise."

Doug turned his back on the woman with the slip strap.

"How is Jason doing in your classroom?"

Ella was surprised by what sounded like genuine concern.

"He's a bit distracted to be quite honest."

"He's that way at home too. I'm a little worried."

Ella looked at Doug Elderby carefully. If he was playing the role of the caring parent he was doing a damn good job. Suddenly she felt sorry for him.

"You know, he may just be looking for some attention."

"Really?" Doug smiled gently. "I thought kids that age just wanted to be left alone. I know I did."

"You could try asking him." Ella tried to stay away from sounding snide.

"That approach didn't work for me. Perhaps I'm just not very good at it. I think it made me more uncomfortable than it did Jason."

"Perhaps in some way it helped." Ella offered.

"Not noticeably." Doug looked at Ella and smiled. She noticed that he had perfectly straight, white teeth.

"Thank you, Ms. Sinclair. You've been very nice about this."

Ella smiled back. She wondered for a moment why Janice would want to screw Dillard when she had this at home.

"Do you enjoy teaching?" Doug asked.

Ella nodded. "Do you?"

Suddenly they were engaged in a conversation on students and classrooms and expectations. Ella found Doug entertaining and was so absorbed in their talk that she was oblivious to Bruce's return from the malted wine bowl.

He nudged her gently with his arm and extended her glass

to her.

Ella smiled at him.

"Mr. Elderby do you know Bruce Hurowitz?"

They shook hands. They exchanged pleasantries and then Doug moved along to other guests.

Bruce mumbled, "Loser."

"What?"

"He's married, Ella."

"So?"

"So, he shouldn't be coming on to other women."

"He was talking to me about teaching."

"He was thinking about you naked."

"Even if that were true, Bruce, that doesn't mean he was coming on to me."

"I was watching him, Ella."

"Through over-protective eyes, Bruce."

Bruce shrugged. He couldn't deny it, but that didn't change his opinion of Doug's dalliances.

Ella smiled. She was amused by her own irrational pleasure at Bruce's jealousy. It was incredibly sexy. Male posturing wasn't normally her thing, but the way Bruce had just sort of placed himself there, rather close to Ella, with that "I'm not buying it" look; well, somehow it was just adorable.

"Just don't get annoyed with me when the roles are reversed and I get in between you and some woman when she's putting the moves on you."

"What makes you think you'll be around?"

"Oh, I'll be around."

Bruce smiled. "Yeah?"

He put his arm around her.

"You're jealousy doesn't bother me. I think it's cute."

"Yeah, but would you think it's cute when it ruins your chance of getting laid?"

Ella was enjoying the arm around her shoulders.

"If it's you ruining my chances, beautiful, I don't mind. 'Course, any time you want to make this less complicated, just let me know."

Ella watched Bruce's lips move. His hand was resting lightly on her shoulder, his fingers playing with the ends of her hair. He had looked so handsome when he picked her up earlier that evening in gabardine pants and a suit jacket. She hadn't really noticed any one as handsome as Bruce at the party. Now she didn't notice any one else at the party period. For Ella they were the only two there.

"I think I want to make it less complicated right now." Ella murmured.

Bruce's surprise didn't detain his retort for more than a second.

"Well, let's go."

Ella stayed silent smiling at him.

Bruce took a deep breath and grinned at her.

"Your hormones are getting the best of you."

"Maybe. So?"

"So I think I'll listen when you've slept off that wine and taken a cold shower. If you're still singing the same tune."

"You know I probably won't be. This may be your only chance, Bruce."

"Yeah? Ya think?" Bruce didn't like the turn the conversation had taken.

Ella shrugged. "Could be. You gonna be decent, do the decent thing?"

She moved closer to him and whispered, "C'mon, handsome, let's go home."

Bruce licked his lips. His throat was dry. She smelled so good. She looked so good. He could hold her, hold her all night long, make love to her, make love until they couldn't stay awake, and then they'd sleep, she in his arms, wrapped up in each other.

"Is this a test, Ella?"

"No test."

Ella stared at him. "This is a one shot deal."

Bruce stared back at her for a long minute. His id and ego fought furiously. He hoped for the answer to spring from Ella's expression. He searched her eyes for a sign, any sign. Could this be the start? Might she change her mind or would this really be a one shot deal? But Ella's face remained impassive. A tiny smile sat on her lips, her eyes bright and challenging.

Bruce swallowed. "I don't want a one shot deal."

Ella ran her hand down Bruce's jacket lapel.

"Feeling a little used, handsome?"

He watched her.

"A little."

"You know what we're passing up? You're clear on this?"

Bruce turned his palms up and shrugged.

"I won't give you a one shot deal. And even if I did, Ella," he glanced at her and smiled, "you'd come back for more."

"Ooooh, good one!" Ella grinned.

"I'm so glad you could make it, Ms. Sinclair," a smooth voice announced behind her.

Ella swung around.

"Oh, hi, Ms. Elderby." Ella was annoyed at the interruption.

Janice glanced at the couple. She smiled slightly.

"I'm sorry, did I interrupt something?"

Her voice is as smooth as butter, Ella thought. She watched Janice give Bruce a sidelong glance.

Bruce introduced himself and Janice said, "Of course you are. I haven't seen you up this close in years. I think the last time we had a conversation you were sixteen."

Bruce knew he was being baited.

"Yeah. I remember. You haven't changed a bit."

Janice gave a delicate laugh and said, "You're very charming."

Oh, VERY charming! Ella thought.

Watching Bruce flirt with other women didn't sit well. And look at Janice, she thought. What's she doing? Janice had called Bruce a child. Now she had absolutely engulfed him in some inconsequential conversation about golf. Well he obviously wasn't too much of a child at this moment. At least she didn't seem to mind if he was. Ella's thoughts were beginning to babble as the wine had taken effect. She stood scowling at them.

A fat lady in a purple, flowing, tent shaped gown, passed them and whispered to Ella, "You're being terribly obvious, honey."

Ella looked at her but she had already passed and moved away.

Ella removed the scowl until she glanced back at Bruce and Janice still in animated conversation and it involuntarily popped back onto her forehead.

She went to the malt wine bowl and replenished her cup.

Where is Doug when you need him, she thought.

"You're gonna have a bodacious hang-over in the morning."

Ella swung around. "Dan!"

He grinned.

"What are you doing here?"

"I'm my Mom's date. And I knew you and Bruce were gonna be here so I thought it might not be a total drag. But hey, I was wrong."

He lowered his voice. "I hate this shit," meaning the party. "You guys plan to stay for long?"

Ella looked at Bruce still talking to Janice.

"I'm all for leaving."

"Great. Get Bruce and let's go."

"What about your Mom?"

Dan waved the question away. "She'll want to stay."

"You go get Bruce." Ella said to Dan as she went to go find her other host.

She touched Doug's arm.

"Thank you, Doug, um, Mr. Elderby."

He smiled. "Doug's fine, Ella. Are you leaving already?"

"Yeah. I have to get up early tomorrow."

"Well it was a pleasure for me. I hope we can talk more often now that we've been properly introduced."

Ella giggled. "It seems so simple."

Shit, she thought. What the hell did that mean? This wine was really getting to her. She shrugged at Doug's confused expression and hurried to the door where Dan and Bruce stood waiting for her.

Chapter 12

"You guys want to go home?" Ella asked.

She sat between Dan and Bruce in Bruce's Chevy. Dan had volunteered to sit in the back, but Ella had insisted that he join them in the front. She had whispered loudly, "this way Bruce and I have to sit closer together."

Dan had nodded largely and glanced at Bruce.

She turned to Dan and asked again.

"You want to go home?"

"Not particularly. Bruce?"

He shrugged.

"You got some other plan?"

"Yeah." Ella said. "Let's go to Worcester. To a bar and dance."

"It's ten o'clock, Ella."

"Perfect. But you two are going to have to draw straws for designated driver. I, obviously, can't."

Dan shook his head. "Neither can I."

Bruce and Ella looked at him.

"I can't drive an automatic."

"What?"

Dan shrugged defensively.

Bruce smirked.

"Whatever. I better stay sober anyway."

Ella nudged him and grinned.

It took three bars before Ella found one she felt comfortable in. It was a small place with a small area for dancing, a few tables, fewer chairs, and a stage. They even had a live band, which wasn't common for a Monday night near the end of a semester. But it wasn't busy which made it a pleasant atmosphere. The band played cover songs all night. Typical eighties stuff, with some of the current alternative radio hits. All stuff Ella enjoyed dancing to.

She had no problem convincing Bruce to dance every song with her. He was all over the floor, doing his thing, which was whatever he felt like at that moment. Ella laughed as much as she danced.

Dan was busy picking up on every available woman in the bar. Occasionally he'd convince one of them to join him in dance. But rarely did they dance with him twice in a row.

Ella waited all night for a slow song. When she finally got one she was wrapped her arms around Bruce as soon as the first few bars sounded.

"Dance with me."

He smiled and held her close.

"This party turned out much better than I ever expected it to." Ella told him.

"What'd you expect?"

"Well, I didn't think I'd get to dance with you tonight. I didn't expect to get this close to you. To be held by you."

"It's not working, beautiful." Bruce said hoping that was true.

Ella sighed. "Well, I'll just have to try and try again then, won't I?"

She gazed at him. Bruce stared back and reconsidered his position. Maybe if he did spend the night with her... Maybe he could just kiss her. Just one kiss. How could that hurt? Yeah, what was one kiss?

"C'mon guys, it's 2:00 in the morning. Let's go." Dan tugged on Ella's arm. He'd given up on the women in the bar.

Ella nodded. It was late and she had to get up in the morning. They all did.

So much for the kiss, Bruce thought.

Ella grabbed her coat and they left.

Chapter 13

"So the vagina was not penetrated?"

Chief Morris watched the two expensively dressed detectives peruse the pictures of Katie Merchant's dead body.

"The Coroner's report is right under the mess you made on my desk, boys."

They ignored him.

Morris swiveled his chair around and stared out the small window at the rain. It had been pelting down all day. He'd have to walk home in the rain. In the rain. After dealing with these two fucks all afternoon. Shit.

"What do you think?"

Chief Morris swiveled back. "What?"

"I asked what you think?"

It was the first time his opinion had been requested.

"I think it was a local. Some one who knew Katie and someone who knew the woods."

"It could be our man from Boston expanding his scope. He has an affinity for little girls."

He dropped the picture in front of Morris.

"Ones who look like this."

"Could be." Morris leaned back in his chair. "But I think this wasn't meant to be a murder. And I think it was one of us."

Ella watched her class stream out the door. It was the last one for the day. A long day. Monday. Her head had boomed until lunchtime despite the Advil Steph had given her.

Jason Elderby hadn't been in class at all today. Maybe he was sick or had the Monday blues.

"Whatchya concentrating on?"

Ella jumped at the unexpected intrusion.

Steph alighted at one of the kids' desks and faced her

friend.

"Talk to me, girl."

"You ever notice your students changing over the course of a couple months?"

"Ella, I teach sixth graders. I see my students changing over the course of one period. There is no holding the evils of adolescence back."

"Yeah, but I mean really change. Disintegrate. Fall apart. Like they're getting sucked into a dark hole and no one is there to save them."

"Well, yeah. Some of them. This is when it happens. We're not social workers, Ella. We can't save them. We try to give them a place to learn."

"Steph! I thought of all people you were a save the world type."

"In a general sense, girlfriend. I do what I can for the greater common good."

"Like teach?"

"Like teach."

Ella stared at her attendance book. "That isn't good enough for me. I have to do something. I can't just sit back and accept it as one of the inevitable casualties. I have to do something."

"Well tell me something I don't already know, Ella."

Steph started to get up. "And that is why you have no life of your own. You get way too wrapped up in whatever or whoever you're doing at the time."

Ella opened her mouth to counter.

"No, no. Don't start this argument with me again, girl. If you weren't so caught up in the way things feel all the time you wouldn't be so restless."

Steph was already walking out the door. "Go ahead. Save the world."

Janice waited impatiently for Doug to get home. It was almost nine. Where the hell was he? She didn't really care where he was or with whom, she just wished he'd come home at a reasonable hour tonight.

Jason was gone. He'd taken that grungy black backpack of his and put god knows what in it, taken the money out of the newspaper subscription envelope and left. She had to find him. Her son. Her baby!

Janice grabbed her car keys off the table. The door had swung shut and locked behind her before she remembered her sleeping five year old. She couldn't leave Daniella home alone, and who the hell knew when Doug would be back. She fumbled with the lock and let herself back in the house.

When she came back out again she was carrying a bundle of blankets and stuffed animals with Daniella nestled inside, peacefully oblivious to the turmoil around her.

She smiled coyly. "Right here on the desk?"

He shrugged. "Why not?"

He ran his hand up the side of her thigh, under her dress, lingering at the curve of her buttocks, brushing his hand lightly back and forth over her silky underwear.

He marveled at her fashion conscious desire to still go bare legged, in a dress, in the chilling November air. It was to his advantage.

"Leave the dress on."

He could feel her slip caressing the back of his hands. Sylvia always wore dresses and the slip was almost always barely visible. It was irresistible.

Sylvia giggled. "O.K., but you've got to promise to make me come with your mouth first if you want to do me from behind."

He propped her up on his desk. With one hand he fumbled with the top buttons of her dress while with the other he fished around behind his back for a couple of chairs for her to put her feet on.

Sylvia enjoyed his struggle. He would reach the chairs eventually. He was headed in the right direction. In the mean time she would let him tickle her nipples with his tongue.

When Sylvia had balanced herself on the edge of the desk, feet up on the back of the chairs, knees bent she whispered, "Pretend I'm at the doctor's office and you're my gynecologist."

A muffled assent came from between her legs. Sylvia smiled when she felt him nod.

Doug wiped the remaining sperm off his penis and tucked

Herman back in his pants. That's what Sylvia had named it. Herman. He watched her button up the last of her buttons and re-adjust the falling slip strap.

"Thanks for all the extra help, professor." She cooed at him.

"Sylvia," he said with his most charming grin, "it's always a pleasure."

Doug stopped by the bathroom on his way out of the liberal arts building. He needed to clean the smell of Sylvia off his mouth. He would eat the granny smith he had saved from lunch on his way home.

Home. He didn't want to go home. He wanted to go to Ella Sinclair's house. He wanted to talk with her, to intellectualize, to pontificate, to drink coffee and argue well into the morning hours about law and circumstance. He didn't even know Ella, didn't know if she had any interest in talking theory until sunrise, but she fascinated him and he felt a connection to her. She inspired those long lost college days feelings that used to make him think the world was his oyster.

He drove nervously toward her house frantically trying out excuses for this uninvited visit on his rear-view mirror.

"...So, then she said just cuz she was late didn't mean she was definitely pregnant. But she's pretty sure she is. She's never been late before. Like clockwork, ya know?"

"What're you gonna do?" Bruce asked solemnly.

Dan shook his head. "I don't know. Wait and see if she really is, I guess."

Bruce leaned forward in his chair.

It was raining again tonight. The air smelled earthy. He and Dan had sat many rainy nights on his porch before watching the lights go on and off in the houses across Summer street. Neither one of them had before ever had a girlfriend who might be pregnant. The whole universe seemed to be descending on North Brooktown.

Bruce watched Ella's house. Her lights were on. She was home. She should be, it was after nine. He would go over there later. To talk to her. To tell her what she was putting him through.

To push her. Maybe to present her with an ultimatum. To make her tell him why Chris had to stand in their way. Maybe to make her give in.

"What if she is pregnant?" Bruce asked. "Have you guys talked about it?"

"No."

"Were you using a condom?"

Dan sighed. "No. She doesn't like the way they feel. I was pulling out."

Bruce looked at his friend. "You want her to have an abortion?"

Dan was silent for a while. "I don't know. I like Jen and I want to have kids some day..."

"What do you think Jen would want?"

Dan shrugged. "She wants to get her Masters' in art history and work in a museum. That's what she talks about. Not having kids."

"What about your plans, man? I thought you wanted to move to Boston after graduation."

"How important is moving to Boston, Bruce? This is a kid we're talking about."

"Maybe. Maybe it's a kid. Maybe it's a bunch of cells. Maybe it's nothing at all."

Dan stared at the rain hitting the street. "Maybe."

Chapter 14

By the time Ella walked in her house it was almost 8:30. She had dinner in a cafe in Brooktown and graded papers. Homemade Macaroni and cheese. It had been palatially well worth the lousy service and annoying draft from the door. And she had read all of the unattended first drafts from last week. Not an unproductive night. Even after she had finished dinner and papers she had lingered, sipping a cafe au lait and contemplating how to tackle the Jason Elderby dilemma.

The direct approach wasn't always successful with angry pre teens. She left the cafe undecided. She would present it to Bruce, see what he had to say.

Dishes. They were stacked six fold in her sink. Crusty, oily, brown and greenish. She dropped her coat on the chair, turned the heat on under the kettle, and set to work on her glasses.

The doorbell rang.

It had to jingle twice before Ella realized the sound was emanating from the front of her house and not the faucet.

Bruce?

She pulled the door open still wiping her hands on her jeans.

Ella stood gaping at her unexpected visitor. Nothing came to her. No thoughts. No salutations. She stood and stared.

There he was. All the way from San Francisco, California to her front door in North Brooktown, Massachusetts.

Ella was speechless and motionless.

Chris smiled slightly.

"Can I come in?"

Ella came to life when he spoke and stepped aside to let him in.

"What are you doing here?"

"I came to see you."

He set his duffel bag by the wall and turned to her.

"I've been trying to call you for a couple weeks. I thought you were going to call me when you got settled."

He glanced around. "You look pretty settled. I see a phone over there. You forget how to dial?"

"I didn't expect you to be sitting anxiously by the phone."

"You didn't think I might be worried about you."

"No. What you might be worrying about wasn't really my number one concern, Chris."

They stared at each other.

"Well I *was* worrying about you. Thinking about you. Everyday."

Ella swallowed. "What the hell made you just show up. Why didn't you call me first?"

"I've been trying, Ella! For two weeks. You're never home. Or you don't answer the phone. Or something."

Ella sighed. "Jesus Christ, Chris."

There was a long silent pause. Then he said softly, "I miss you, Ella."

"You miss me? You *miss* me?" Ella shook her head. "N,n,n,n,n,no. No way, Chris. You're not doing this to me again. You obviously have no clue what getting dumped by you felt like for me. How much it hurt. Or whatever. Maybe you don't give a shit how much it hurt me. I don't know. And I don't care. I'm not...just...no way."'

Chris stared at her. Then he said slowly, "I understand that you feel that way. I know I hurt you and I know I have no right to be here and no right to ask you to give me a second chance. But...," he licked his lips. "But I'm here. And...I think we can make this work. I'm willing to do whatever you want, Ella. You can have it totally your way."

"And that's supposed to make it O.K.?"

Chris just stroked his chin and stood silently staring at her. It was overwhelmingly familiar to her.

"Fuck you, Chris!" Ella pointed her finger at him. "Fuck you! You broke my heart. I trusted you and I believed in us and you made a bunch of bullshit promises and I feel like a fucking fool! I am a fucking fool."

She took a breather. "But I'm getting over it now. I'm dealing with my own shit now. And.... I don't know."

She gazed at him defiantly. "I don't really understand how you can just show up here and expect me to, whatever the hell it is you expect from me."

Chris shrugged and remained silent.

"How could you even come here?"

"It was more like, how could I not come here. You're all I think about, Ella. I know I fucked up. I know I'm going to pay for that. But I'm willing to spend the rest of my life making up for it."

He gave her a minute to let it sink in. "I know you're the best thing that ever happened to me. You're the one. You're the one I want to spend the rest of my life with. I know that now. I realized that about four seconds after you left. I had all that freedom I wanted, and all that space I was looking for and all I could think about was how much I wanted you."

Ella hesitated, "Well, I can't. Just..."

The doorbell rang. Both of them jumped.

Ella stared at the door. She knew who it was. Slowly she pulled it open.

"Hey beauti..." Bruce saw Chris. "...ful."

Ella shut the door behind Bruce and introduced them. Neither one of them said anything.

Bruce nodded.

Chris raised his eyebrows.

Ella sighed.

The doorbell rang again.

"It's a party." Ella announced. "Let them in, would ya, Bruce?"

Doug Elderby stepped around the door. "Ella?"

"Doug?"

"Am I disturbing something?"

"Why no. Does it look that way?"

Bruce scowled at Ella. "Why the hell is this guy stopping by?" Indicating Doug.

Chris turned on Bruce. "What the hell business is it of yours?"

"What the fuck are you doing here anyway?" Bruce returned.

Doug put his palms up. "Sorry, Ella. This is obviously a bad time. I just wanted to talk. I'll come back some other time."

90

"No." Chris announced in his mild way. "You don't need to come back."

Ella snapped at him. "Shut up, Chris."

The phone rang.

Ella dropped her hand on her head. "Fuck me! O.K., don't anybody move. Put your guns back in your holsters while I go answer the phone."

She dashed into the front room and grabbed the screaming receiver.

"Hello?"

"Ella? Janice Elderby. I need your help."

"Are you looking for Doug?" Ella asked.

A brief silence followed. It was the static on the line that made Ella realize she had said the wrong thing.

Then quietly Janice said, "No. But now I know where he is."

"Well, he just got here." Ella defended.

"It doesn't matter, Ella. Really. Jason is gone. That's why I called. My son has run away from home and I need some help."

Ella bellowed, "Doug, get in here and talk to your wife."

Then back into the receiver. "I'll talk with you again after you spoken with Doug."

Ella returned to the hall where Chris and Bruce stood not looking at each other.

She turned to Bruce.

"Jason's run away from home. That was Janice on the phone. Any idea where a distraught kid might go?"

Bruce shook his head.

"The woods maybe. For while. Or a friend's house."

Ella thought for a moment.

"I don't think he has any friends really."

Chris spoke up.

"He might be headed toward Brooktown where he can catch a train or a bus, Hon'."

"Hon'?" Bruce snapped.

Ella glowered at Bruce.

"Think Bruce. I need your help. About Jason."

Bruce sighed.

"There's a place in Foxboro that kids call 'the box'. It's the basement of the old Vets' Hall that hasn't been used for anything for years. You can't be a homeless runaway for long and not hear about it. It's where you can make your connections to Boston. Pimps and dealers and shit."

"He's not there yet. Not if he's just been missing tonight." Chris added.

Ella looked at him.

"You know about this place too?"

He nodded.

She turned back to Bruce.

"Go home. Get Dan and take a look through the woods. The areas you know. Or where you think he might go. Anywhere you guys can think of."

He stared at her.

"O.K. Ella. I'm leaving. But think about what you're doing."

He slammed the door behind him.

It's justified, Ella conceded.

Doug was off the phone.

"Janice said to tell you we'll be searching most of tonight for Jason. But she's making some coffee and getting donuts for the neighbors who have agreed to help. She'd like you to stop by. I think she needs to talk."

Ella nodded.

"I have to go." He hesitated. "I don't know where to start. Looking, I mean."

Chris said, "Just start driving around. See where you end up."

Doug nodded and tried to smile. Ella opened the door for him.

"I'll be over in a few minutes, Doug. Tell Janice." Ella shut the door and turned slowly back to Chris.

"You've been busy making friends. No wonder you didn't have time to call me."

Ella smirked and shook her head.

"Don't even lay a guilt trip on me, Chris. What I've been doing is none of your business."

"You're right. But I still feel like it is. I haven't been doing anything except thinking about you. I haven't been seeing anyone. I don't want to see anyone. I want to be with you. And I think... fuck we don't have time for this right now."

"No, you're right we don't."

Ella started to turn toward the door. Chris grabbed her arm. "Hey, I think we can work it out."

"We don't have time to talk about this right now, Chris. We've got to help the Elderby's. You up for it?"

"Yeah." Chris reached for his jacket. "Let's go."

"I knew he was unhappy. I just didn't know what to do about it. I didn't know what approach to take. Kids can be so resistant. I just..." Janice stared out the window.

Ella poured more milk in her coffee. They never put enough in. When she let other people doctor up her coffee they never put enough in.

"Nobody knows what to do, Janice. I guess you just try things. Sometimes you get lucky. I think all relationships are like that." Ella wondered if any of her pop psych was consoling. Unlikely.

Janice ignored her.

"I don't cry. I've never been a crier. I always thought it was a sign of weakness in women. Women that cried always made me want to give them a lesson in self respect and a hardy slap on the mouth."

Shit! Ella thought, but remained silent.

"I know you think I'm a lousy slut for my affair with John. Maybe I am. Maybe I'm a shitty wife. And that's my fault. I don't try anymore. I don't care anymore." She paused and stared into her mug. "But I always tried to be a good mother. I love my children."

"Janice, why did Paulie Turtino kill himself?"

Janice glanced up surprised.

"I don't know. I suppose he was unhappy."

Panic welled up in her eyes. "You don't think..."

"No." Ella jumped on that one. "Every kid is confused somewhere along the line. Most of them don't commit suicide."

Janice rubbed her forehead.

Ella watched her chic red fingernails dig into the skin around the bridge of her nose. Her make up was still intact, even under the eyes. She hadn't cried. Or she bought really expensive make up. Maybe both.

"Why did Dillard replace the other priest? I mean, isn't that unusual: for a small, conservative town to oust their priest?"

Janice studied Ella. "You sound like a smut reporter digging for a story."

Fuckin' A! Ella thought. I'm trying to help the bitch! O.K., she's scared. Her son split, her husband cheats, or wants to, and she's fucking a priest. Her life sucks. Give her a break.

"It might help to figure things out. There might be some connections here." Ella's voice was pedantic.

Janice looked skeptical.

"Gossip strikes me as undignified." She was mumbling.

"Janice."

"O.K., he was discovered to have a lover."

Ella waited.

"A man. The janitor. They were caught together in his office."

What is it with sex in churches? Ella almost said it aloud.

"The town ostracized him for that?"

"Like you said, it's a conservative town."

"If he'd been caught with a woman?"

Janice shrugged. "It probably would've been O.K."

If it'd been a woman he would've gotten a thump on the back. And for those who really did take his vow of celibacy seriously it would've been accepted as a natural and forgivable temptation. Women, sin, temptation. Ella shook her head. Catholicism was mystifying. Terrifying.

"I'm going back out. Staying here is driving me crazy." Janice dropped her mug into the sink.

"I think what Doug said about someone being home makes sense. If Jason does come back you should be here. Some one should be here."

"Well you stay then."

Before Ella could protest Janice had grabbed her ski jacket and rushed out the door.

Ella listened to Janice's car pull out of the driveway. She glanced at the clock. It was shortly before Eleven. School tomorrow. It was unlikely that she would be home before the morning hours. She let out a sigh and rested her head on her arm. Time to think.

Chapter 15

Galvin Zipher stepped around the pile of dog feces that was left surreptitiously on one side of the sidewalk. Parker sniffed at it lethargically.

Galvin smiled. The older dogs got the less interested they seemed to become in other dogs' bodily functions. All fascinations seemed to mellow with age.

"C'mon Parker." Galvin called.

He took the small path leading into the woods.

Parker bounded in front of him. He knew the way. They'd been doing this for years.

Suddenly the dog came to a complete stop. He stood perfectly still, his tail up, ears perked. Galvin stopped also. He knew well enough to trust his dog's instincts. Galvin was so still that his breathing seemed to boom within him.

Both dog and Master heard the rustling of a leaf. The dog began to bark furiously. Then Galvin heard a scream.

A sobbing voice yelled, "Don't hurt me. Don't let him hurt me."

It was a child's voice.

Galvin quieted his dog and went over to the boy.

Jason Elderby's face peered at him from underneath a large evergreen bush.

"What are you doing here, son?"

"Hiding."

"Why?"

Jason didn't answer.

Galvin recognized that the boy was trying not to cry.

"C'mon." He said gently. "Let's take you home."

Dan and Bruce showed up in Janice's kitchen shortly after midnight.

"Well?" Ella asked as she proffered coffee.

"Nothing."

Bruce took off his jacket and sat down.

Dan joined him.

"If he's hiding in the woods he's doing a good job of it."

"Well, he hasn't come back. Neither has anyone else."

"Where's Chris?"

Bruce took a bite of a donut.

Ella sighed.

"Not now, Bruce."

"Sure, Ella. Whenever you want. Whatever you want. You gotta do your thing. Don't let me fuck that up."

"Don't start in on her now, dude."

"Shut up, Dan."

Dan smiled and shook his head.

"Relax, buddy." He got up. "I'm going home. I'm not going to be able to find that kid tonight. You want a ride home?" He looked at his friend.

Bruce shook his head. "I'll walk."

"Thanks anyway, Dan." Ella said.

Dan gave her a smile as he left.

Ella glanced back at Bruce. He was staring at her.

"Why's he here, Ella? Does he want to take you back to San Francisco with him?"

"He's here because he realized he made a mistake."

"*He* made a mistake? I thought you left him."

Ella shook her head.

After a moment she said, "Look Bruce, I don't see why we even need to talk about it. I've got some things to figure out. That's all."

"You don't see why we need to talk about it? You can't think of any reason why I deserve an explanation?"

He waited.

"Fuck! This fucking sucks, Ella. This fucking sucks."

Ella sighed and put her hands on her hips. "O.K., what do you want to know, Bruce?"

"What happened? What was his mistake?"

"He just stopped being in love with me I guess. He got distant. And when I got a job here it was the perfect excuse to split up. At first he didn't want me to go. But then he was afraid to ask me to stay because then he'd be responsible to me. Finally he ended up saying he needed his space anyway so I might as well take the job if I really wanted it."

Ella was staring at her mug.

"Go on."

Softer and with more hesitation this time she said, "I begged him not to dump me. But he did. And I cried and felt betrayed, hoping to all hell that he'd regret it, and packed my bags and here I am."

"Well you got what you were hoping for, didn't you?"

Ella glanced at Bruce.

"I guess I provided a pretty good diversion while you were waiting for your little buddy to 'regret it'. You were thinking "Yeah. I'll fuck around with Bruce for a while. He's in love with me, he'll do anything I want." It's real nice to have some one be in love with you isn't it, Ella? It just makes you feel all…wanted. And you're real good at keeping 'em right there. You know? In that special place where they never really know. Give them just enough. Keep them hoping."

Ella swallowed. Bruce scooted his chair out.

"You didn't tell me any lies, Ella. That's your big talent. You don't tell lies. But you miss the truth by a long shot."

"It's called deception, Bruce."

Bruce raised his eyebrows. He leaned back in his chair, shook his head, closed his eyes. Ella watched the move as if it were a dance. A gentle, sardonic smile, a smile of disbelief played on his lips. Her heart lurched forward and got caught in her throat. Bruce had never been anything but sweet to her. Sweet and loving.

Suddenly Bruce was up and moving towards the door, jacket in hand. He had it open a crack before Ella got there to slam it shut and place herself in front of it.

She hugged him fiercely.

"Don't walk away from me like this, Bruce. I'm sorry I said that deception thing, it just came out."

Her words were slightly muffled by his shoulder and arm where she was nestling her head.

"It's not as simple as you think. Not since you complicated things. And you did. You complicated things."

Slowly Bruce put his arms around Ella. The hug tightened

for a second.

The knock on the door made them both jump.

"Shit!" They said it in unison.

"That scared the crap out of me." Ella breathed.

She opened the door. There stood Galvin with Jason. Bruce moved around Ella and pulled Jason inside the house.

"Welcome home, kid. You look pretty cold. C'mon." He maneuvered the boy into the kitchen.

Ella listened to Galvin's explanation. He rejected her offer of coffee. Parker was waiting patiently outside. He had just wanted to drop Jason safely at home. No, he didn't want to wait around for Janice or Doug to return. He and Parker were going to go on home now. Galvin was certain Ella could pass on what little he knew competently.

Ella shut the door behind him. She heard the two male voices from the kitchen. Jason was telling hesitantly of his adventure in the woods as he stirred his hot chocolate.

Ella watched Bruce. He looked so attentive, but without seeming intrusive. It seemed to work for Jason. Why not? It had worked on her. Whatever charm Bruce oozed, it had definitely been effective.

Now the night could wind down. The chase was over.

Ella went into the kitchen to wait for the rest of the posse.

Bruce looked at her.

"You O.K.?"

She nodded.

Jason had finished his hot chocolate and was dozing in front of the Television. Reruns of "Bewitched" danced in the background.

"Where's he sleeping tonight, Ella?"

She shook her head.

"It's driving me crazy. You know that? It's driving me fucking crazy."

"You have to back off, Bruce. I have to spend some time with him. I have to!"

"Yeah, now. Now when it's convenient. Now, I have to back off, Ella. And when you change your mind, you'll come and get me, right?"

"You're free to make those choices yourself, Bruce. It's not just what I want. I'm not the only fucking person who has things to decide."

"Right, Ella. I have to decide whether I love you enough to let you screw me over with your ex-boyfriend."

Ella closed her eyes and rubbed her temples.

"Maybe I just need you to trust me on this. Right now I need you to trust me."

Bruce pulled his cap off, smoothed his hair back, and pulled his cap back on. Ella had witnessed this routine many times in the short month she'd known him. It was a sign of contemplation, of consideration.

"You need me to be your friend. You need me to trust you."

Ella waited for him to make his point.

"You want me to love you, Ella. You're making sure that I don't let go of that cuz then you'll have nothing. If this thing with Chris doesn't work out you want to be able to turn to me. Well, it's not that easy. I'm not that easy. If you want me, you're going to have to decide that now. Even though now is a bad time. You're gonna have to want me now."

The door opened and Janice walked in with Chris and Chief Morris. She looked at Ella hopefully. Ella pointed to the living room.

Chris waited long enough to hear Janice's cry of relief before he turned to Ella.

"Ready to go?"

She glanced at Bruce. He stared back at her.

"Yeah."

Chapter 16

Ella pulled up in front of the cafe Norde in Brooktown. Just a quick au lait and she'd be on her way. She had a good half hour before she needed to be in her classroom.

She turned her engine off and sat for a moment in the car.

Ella closed her eyes and let the persistent image of Chris' body lying back on her bed, slightly tense, frowning with concentration, beads of sweat on his forehead, his heavy breathing, his hands firmly moving her hips a mere fraction back and forth against his own minute movement. The memory made her warm.

She cracked the window in the car and gave her head a shake.

The sex had been incredible. It usually was with Chris. But the aftermath felt different this time. She hadn't slipped into a deep and comforting sleep. She had lain awake in his arms and wondered what she would say to Bruce. Even what she would say to Chris.

Their love-making had not been the result of the resolution of their problems. It had come suddenly, in the middle of things.

They had started trying to talk things over. Neither one of them was able to go to sleep after their event-filled night, nor could they ignore the excitement of seeing each other again. Ella had been able to put aside her resentment and they talked about Chris' realizations.

It hadn't taken him long, he claimed, to realize that he had misunderstood his anxiety. He had blamed the one thing in his life that was least responsible for his inner turmoil, their relationship. He thought if he were just free of the responsibility of another person's feeling then he would no longer feel confused or stifled. Everything should've fallen in place when he got his independence back. And then, of course, once Ella was really gone, he recognized his confusion for what it was, his. Something he had to figure out, something within, something far more personal than ever could be brought about or disposed of by another human being. But the worst of it was that the best thing that he had ever experienced was now no longer part of his life.

Chris said he'd waited as long as he could for Ella to contact him. He reminded her that she'd promised to get in touch with him a lot earlier. He thought he was dignifying her request for some time to deal with her own emotions before she re-established any interaction between them. He had wanted to call her, to fly out to her, a week after she left. But he waited. He waited to give her the time she'd demanded. Now he wished he hadn't. Now, he said, he saw why the phone call hadn't and hadn't come.

Ella replied, "You dumped me, Chris. No guilt trips." Everything Chris said was soothing for Ella's ego, but it was when he began professing his desire to be with her, his complete willingness to leave San Francisco behind and be with her in the environment that made her happiest that the conversation became seductive to Ella.

It was in the middle of this that Ella kissed him. Chris' exposition went no further. It was a matter of a few minutes before their clothing was littering her living room and staircase and they were moving slowly, naked, together, on her bed.

"So you fucked him?" Steph put down her sandwich.

Ella nodded. "Yeah, I fucked him."

"What about Bruce?"

Ella stared at the table. "I don't know, woman. I just don't know. I feel I have to tell him, yet on the other hand it isn't exactly any of his business."

"If you tell him, how do you think he'll react? No, no, no. Better yet; how do you *want* him to react?"

"I'm not being malicious, Steph. I'm not fucking Chris to make Bruce jealous."

"Heaven help you if you were, honey." Steph took a bite of her sandwich and waved away any rationalizing Ella might do while she chewed.

"So," she said when she'd swallowed, "you've got your pick of these two men, both ones you like, and you don't know what to do. You don't really want to chose cuz that would mean acting instead of reacting to involvement and you hate to do that, so you're gonna leave one of 'em hanging so that he'll leave you behind and then you can be with the other one without ever suffering the consequences of choice."

"I don't think I'm doing that, Steph."

Steph scrunched up her face and moved her shoulders back and forth mimicking, "I don't think I'm doing that, Steph."

Ella laughed. "They're both great. I was pretty hooked on Chris until I met Bruce. I mean, I really thought I was keeping it under control, but now I'm not so sure I just want to give Bruce up to be with Chris again. This is everything I wished for a couple months ago. But I'm not sure anymore. I feel ambivalent."

"To say the least."

Ella sighed.

Steph looked at her. "Tell me something, Ella, what do you really want from these two? Are you going to marry one of them? Do you want either one of them to really rely on you as someone in their future? Someone they're actually going to be able to count on? C'mon girl, what are you doing?"

"I don't see why I have to think about that stuff, Steph. I don't see why I can't simply follow through on what feels good right now."

"Yes you do, Ella. And if you pretend not to you're a fool!"

"That's your perspective, Steph, because that kind of thing is important to you and therefore you think it's important to everybody, but it isn't. A lot of people, yes, but I'm not one of them, and for all we know neither are Chris and Bruce."

"That is utter bullshit and you know it. You know as well as I do that my perspective is shared by both Bruce and Chris. You don't have to admit it to me, I don't care. But for God's sake, girl, don't pretend like you aren't cheating and deceiving those two out of something you know is important to them just because it suits you to have them around. If you really want the freedom you say you want find someone who wants the same thing and let the rest of them alone!"

"They are both adults, Stephanie. I think they can make up their minds for themselves. I've never pretended to be interested in anything more than a relationship, however intimate. But I'm not about to limit myself to some immature middle-ager with an identity crisis who can't make an emotional commitment simply because you think I'm responsible for the expectations of the men I get involved with."

"You are such a coward, Ella! You *are* responsible for the expectations of the men you get involved with. That's what getting involved is all about."

"Then by the same token, they are responsible to my expectations as well."

"Yeah. And you expect to eat your cake and have it too."

"Steph, that is completely unfair! You only see it that way because you think marriage and family are everything."

"We are *not* talking about me. We are talking about the two men you are stringing along. You fucked Chris last night. What do you think he's going to think that means? What, Ella? Is he going to think it was a good-bye fuck, you're out of my life now but I wanted something to masturbate to on the slow days? No. He's going to think that he stands a pretty good chance of getting you back. And what about Bruce? What's he going to think? Oh, she just needed to get the whole sex-with-Chris thing out of her system. After this she's all mine. Yeah? Or might Bruce think that since you're fucking your ex he's out of the picture. And moreover, what do you want them to think? Are you even going to leave them alone long enough to get over this mess and move on?"

Steph pointed her finger.

"You are not so altruistic, girlfriend. None of us are, but at least some of us don't try to convince ourselves we are. You are deciding what is going to happen. Passively I admit, but none-the-less."

Ella opened her mouth, but Steph waved her protestations away.

"Whatever, Ella. I don't have to mend a broken heart. You do whatever you want. But don't pretend to me that you don't know exactly what you're doing. I don't want to hear no complaints when this blows up in your face."

Ella dropped her hands on her knees.

"Well then who the hell am I going to complain to? I can't afford therapy."

Steph smiled and shook her head.

"Uh huh. You make light of it, honey. Go ahead."

Ella grinned and squeezed Steph's hand.

"You'll always listen to me, Stephanie, and you know it. Cuz, my hectic life keeps you happy with yours. You and Jon wouldn't be nearly so smug if it weren't for my craziness."

"You think?"

Ella nodded.

"Besides you want to know who I'm going to end up with."

"Girl, you gonna end up alone!"

Ella rolled her eyes.

"Well thanks for the vote of confidence. I'll keep your advice, if that's what it was, in mind."

Chapter 17

John Dillard pulled open the third file drawer. He was nearing the end of this dreary task. It was exceptionally uninviting to him to organize and file, so he'd left the burden of rearranging his predecessor's papers until three months after his arrival. Now he was almost finished.

He still had a meeting of the Foxboro Boys and Girls club to attend this evening, so he had to get moving.

Dillard finished the task and gave the file drawer a kick. It swung into place, met resistance and swung back out again. John caught himself about to emit a blue steak longer than any man of the cloth should indulge in.

He shoved his hand in toward the back of the drawer and pulled out the obstruction. One more file. Untitled. John flipped it open. He stared at the words on the first sheet, "my love…"

So many priests had their sins, Dillard mused. Hester Prine's prince wasn't the only clergyman who could piously indulge in a touch of self-flagellation.

Dillard studied with horrified fascination the angry love letter in front of him. It made his own behavior seem almost laughable.

It was forty minutes later and he was late for the club meeting by the time he reached the end of the stack of letters. He shoved the file in his briefcase and hurried out of the church.

"I'd really like to talk to him for a few minutes, Ms. Elderby."

Chief Morris stood firmly planted on the Elderby's front stoop. "I really don't see why that's necessary, Chief. Jason's had a very exhausting experience and if you don't mind I'd like to let things get back to normal."

"I don't mind things getting back to normal, Ms. Elderby, but I think Jason might have some information about Katie Merchant that he needs to unload. I think that might be the only road back to normal for that youngster."

"According to what evidence, Mr. Morris?"

"No evidence, Mam. Just a hunch."

"Well your hunches mean nothing to me, Chief. I'm sorry that the case with Katie is unresolved, but I think my son's welfare takes precedence over your career plans. Now if you'll excuse me, I need to attend to my family."

The door slammed shut in Morris' face. He sighed and turned slowly around. He took a moment to breathe in deeply the cold, late autumn, morning air.

There was no denying it, the Elderby's had a lovely plot of land. Their front yard included a spot of woods on either side of their driveway. He knew well enough that in the late spring their early blooming roses were spectacular, but this time of year there was no contesting the beauty of their colorful trees. Even this late in the season the Elderby's still had a blaze of red and orange and brown glowing in the morning sunlight. Morris considered his life. He hadn't been many places. Never to another country. But of what he'd seen, this was the most beautiful place on earth. North Brooktown in the fall.

His doctor had told him, "Look around you, Fenton. Stop and look around."

Morris watched a burning orange leaf flutter to the ground. Winter was approaching. And doc was right. One heart attack was enough. Katie Merchant was dead. Getting Jason Elderby to talk wouldn't bring her back. It wouldn't deliver Katie back into Ruth's arms. Or Alwin's for that matter. Mercy.

Bruce swung the ax down and split the log in half. He hadn't chopped wood in two years. They usually bought their wood chopped. Chopped and delivered. But for some reason, today he felt like chopping his own wood. He'd been at it for hours. Two hours. Bruce could feel the ache in this shoulders and back, but he didn't want to stop. Don't stop, don't think.

"Bruce!"

Bruce swung around and saw Dan approaching with Ella in tow.

"Look who I found knockin' on your front door."

Bruce rested the ax on his shoulder and looked at Ella.

"Hey Bruce." Ella fidgeted under his gaze.

"Hey Ella."

"How are you?"

"How do you think?"

Ella gave a small shrug.

"I haven't heard from you in two days, Ella. What's been going on?"

"I don't know exactly. I mean, it's all still sort of a mess."

"Then what are you doing here? Go home. Go back to your little buddy. Isn't he going to get suspicious if you're out here talking to me?"

"He's in Worcester visiting his Uncle."

"Ohhh. Well, in that case, come on in. Maybe we can make out for a while before he gets back. As long as you're home before he is."

"Fuck you, Bruce."

Ella started to stomp off. Dan grabbed her arm while Bruce retorted, "Whatever you say, Ms. Sinclair. No, let her go Dan."

"Just hang on a second, Ella." Dan said with a firm grip on her arm. "I want to talk to both of you and I don't want to say the same shit twice."

Ella looked suspicious.

Dan said, "This is about Paulie Turtino."

He let go of Ella's arm and continued. "I think he was being abused. My Mom said something about that last night, how kids in a small town don't have the resources that kids might have in Boston. When I asked her what she meant she said 'look at the Turtino boy'. She said she thought his parents were beating up on him."

The three of them stood in silence.

Finally Ella piped up, "It's all pretty obvious I think. Just none of us want to face it."

Bruce nodded. "Yeah. But there's nothing we can do about it now."

"How can we not do anything about it?" Ella sounded incensed.

"It's just stirring up a hornet's nest, El." Dan defended.

Bruce nodded. "Yeah. And no one's going to admit anything

at this point."

"Well, I think those are cop-outs. Lousy fucking cop-outs. Besides, Jason Elderby might well go admitting stuff if he feels like it's O.K. to talk."

Bruce and Dan looked confused.

"Jason Elderby? What's he got to do with this?"

Ella slapped her hand to her forehead. "C'mon guys, THINK!"

"Explain."

"I don't have time to explain. I've got to go."

"Where? Where are you off to now?"

"To see Dillard." Ella called over her retreating shoulder.

Dan turned to Bruce. "Why?"

Bruce shrugged. "I don't know. But we've got somewhere to go to. I just thought of this. C'mon."

"Where?"

"You'll see."

"What are we gonna do?"

"Improvise."

Ella stepped up to Fr. Dillard's office and knocked on the door. His nameplate advertised his degrees in higher education. He was a Ph.D. Ella hadn't realized that before. She had enough time before he answered her summons to wonder how stimulating North Brooktown could be to a man of books and letters. She got her intellectual snobbery in check just before the door swung open.

"Ms. Sinclair!"

"Mr. Dillard. May I come in?"

He nodded and stepped aside. Ella walked past him and wondered if he thought this was his lucky day.

His office was tiny and disheveled. Books and papers everywhere. Ella felt momentarily at ease. The late afternoon sun was shining in his one window and the big, shabby chair she plopped down in was cozy.

"A cup of tea?"

Ella waved away the offer.

"No thank you. Actually, I don't want to stay long. I just want a few questions answered."

Dillard raised his eyebrows.

"I know the priest here before you was gay. I know that he was caught with his lover. But I want you to tell me why he left. Why he was kicked out."

"It seems to me like you have all the answers already, Ms. Sinclair."

"No, Mr. Dillard. I know that is not the extent of it. I know there is more to it."

"Then you know more than I."

Ella watched him. "Did you know Jason Elderby ran away from home?"

"Yes. I'd heard. But from what I gather he's home now and doing fine."

"He's in your choir. Did you notice anything? Did he seem different? Upset as of late?"

"He's in your class. Did you?"

Ella sighed. "I need to know why Father Muldoon was ostracized. If he had any unconventional sexual practices I need you to tell me what they were."

"You sound like quite the young sensationalist, Ms. Sinclair. And kind of nosy."

"You're kind of high-handed for someone protecting a secret, aren't you?"

"Is that a threat?"

Ella hesitated. Could it be?

"No. Look… No, it's not a threat. Your affairs are your affairs." She smiled at her own cleverness. "I just want to get some things straightened out. I think it'll be better this way in the long run. Especially for Jason."

"I think Jason will be fine. He has an upstanding family who will protect him and make sure he doesn't cause any more trouble. He has a good home. He'll be back in the parish again and God will take care of the rest.

Ella was about to express a contradictory opinion when he said, "Sometimes it is better to let sleeping dogs lie."

Ella snorted softly and shook her head.

"Is that what you spent all those years learning when you got your Ph.D.? To let sleeping dogs lie? You learned that ignoring the problem will make it go away? Don't talk about it and it won't be there?"

"I learned to put my faith in God."

"Whatever."

Dillard stared at her.

"Why are you so angry with the church? Or is it God you resent?"

Ella stood up.

"Yeah, I really need to be psycho-analyzed by a Priest. I'm leaving."

Dillard grabbed her hand.

"Ella, spirituality, belief; those are good things. They can help. Everyone needs to believe that things will work out the way they should sometimes."

"They don't work out the way they should sometimes, John. If Paulie Turtino was being molested by Muldoon, so might Jason have been. Paulie obviously didn't believe things were going to work out the way they should, did he now?"

"Jason might. Jason's family does."

"Yeah right. When is the last time you really listened to Janice?"

"You can't solve other people's problems. There will always be the poor and forsaken and lonely. The best you can do is count your blessings and try to live your life as nobly as possible."

"And put my faith in God?"

"Put your faith in something, Ella."

"This conversation doesn't seem the least bit hypocritical to you?"

"It is wiser not to judge other people's choices."

"As long as those choices don't include sexually abusing alter boys."

"Do you plan to single handily exterminate evil, Ms. Sinclair?"

"I obviously plan to do more about it than you do."

"And you're not the least bit concerned that you might be jumping to conclusions? And what effect that might have? This is a small town. People aren't as accustomed to having accusations hurled at them as they might be in San Francisco. The results, whatever they are, might be devastating."

"If Jason was molested I can guarantee you that the results will be devastating."

"If."

Ella pulled her arm gently away from Dillard's grip.

"You just keep living in your sheltered world where the just God brings about all retribution one fine day. It's much easier than the guilt of uncertainty. You've been no help at all, John. Not to me, and in my opinion, not to Jason. Certainly not to Paulie."

Dillard looked away from her momentarily. Then his gaze met hers.

"I would have liked to have been. Your burden seems heavier than it should be."

Ella scowled. "I can handle it."

Chapter 18

Bruce propped his arm up on the counter.

"O.K. Cabbot. She thinks she figured it out. She said to run this by you and see if it was right."

"Why didn't she come down here herself?"

"Cuz you're a slimy bastard and she doesn't want to deal with you."

Cabbot laughed. "Maybe that was your idea."

"Maybe. Anyway, do you want to hear her theory or not?"

"Sure."

"Paulie Turtino hanged himself because his Dad molested him. Being catholic and all he couldn't tell anyone cuz your parents can do no wrong."

"That's half-baked."

Bruce and Dan and Cabbot stared at each other.

"Well?" Dan asked. "Is her theory the same as yours?"

"No."

Bruce snorted. He'd been holding his breath.

Cabbot slowly continued, "But she's not that far off. Only, give the Catholics a little more misguided martyrdom and you'll get it."

Ella listened to Dan finish his tale. The last of the afternoon sun was beating down as fervently as a November sun could muster still managing to make all the trees behind the stone ridge along county route 161 seem ablaze. The last of the autumn leaves always burned the brightest shades of orange and gold.

"It's going to be winter soon. Look at how bare the trees are getting."

Dan stared at her. "We're telling you about Cabbot and Paulie and theories and shit, and you're talking about winter?"

Ella looked past Dan to Bruce.

"What do you think, Bruce? Did the priest molest Paulie? Is that the straw that broke the camel's back?"

"I think if that isn't it, it's not far from it."

Ella thought for a moment.

"I never knew Cabbot was so literate. That whole misguided martyrdom thing, that's pretty good. What makes Cabbot despise Catholicism so much anyway? Or is it all religion?"

"No. It's Catholicism. He told me I'm O.K. cuz I'm a Jew." Bruce told her.

"It's odd. It's such an unusual prejudice. How does he feel about you Dan? You're Catholic."

"Sounds like we made more head way than you did." Dan intruded into Ella's musings entirely ignoring her question.

"Yeah. You did. But you know, that whole scene just served to make me even more certain that I'm right. And that Dillard knows it."

She glanced at them. "So what do we do now?"

Dan stood up.

"We go home. I've got to meet Jen at Planned Parenthood."

"You want me to come with you?" Bruce asked.

Dan shook his head.

"Why? What's going on?" Ella demanded.

"Jen thinks she might be pregnant."

Ella's mouth dropped open and she stared at Dan.

"When did you find this out? Why didn't you say anything?"

"I guess Bruce tried to let you in on it."

Ella looked at Bruce.

He shrugged. "You've been preoccupied." To Dan, "Are you O.K.?"

Dan grabbed Ella's arm and pulled her upright.

"C'mon let's go. I'm fine. So's Jen."

"Have you guys decided what you're going to do if she is?"

"Nope."

Ella glanced at Bruce. He smiled slightly and gave her a gentle wink. It was a reassuring gesture to Ella, and she put her hand to her heart and grinned.

In a bold move she linked her arm through his and he gave it a squeeze.

"So, what's the deal with us, Ella?"

Bruce walked next to her their arms still linked. They had sent Dan on home alone in the car. They wanted to talk and walk and be alone together.

"I don't know exactly, Bruce."

"Well what's going through your mind?"

Ella hesitated.

"I wish I could have both relationships. I still love Chris. And now he's finally in love with me. And he's here to prove it. But I want to give you and I a chance. I don't want to give you up for Chris. Not even for Chris. I used to think I'd give up just about anything for Chris, but I don't feel that way anymore. I don't want to let you go, Bruce."

Bruce stopped and faced her. "I can't go there, Ella. I won't go there. You can't have it both ways. I'm not gonna share you."

"Bruce..."

"Would you share me with someone? If Terri showed up in town and wanted to get back together would you be O.K. with that?"

Ella shook her head slowly. "No. Not a chance."

"Look what you're asking for, Ella." Bruce said quietly.

Ella sighed loudly.

"This is exactly what I was trying to avoid. This whole mess. This whole complication! This is why I thought we should just be friends. If we had just kept this whole relationship in check from the beginning none of this would have ever happened."

"What the hell is so great about this guy anyway? Why avoid this? Why are you letting me go for him? He dumped you, Ella. So, fuck him. He made that choice. I'm not going to do that. He fucked up. So let it be over now. Give *this* relationship a chance."

Ella closed her eyes.

"What are you doing?"

"I'm willing this whole thing away. When I open my eyes all decisions will be made for me and everything else will have disappeared. Or rather, everything will be back to normal."

"Send him home, beautiful."

Ella opened her eyes and looked at him.

"Send him home," Bruce repeated, "or it really is over between us."

Ella stepped cautiously up to the entrance of the Police Department in Brooktown. They were a division of Worcester County PD but everyone in the area thought of them as the local cops. Chief Morris actually lived in North Brooktown, so the case was doubly important to him.

Ella had managed to squeeze in an appointment with him when she had called from the school that morning. At first Morris was hesitant, but he granted her an audience when she told him she thought she might know something about the Katie Merchant case.

"Well Ms. Sinclair, you're here and I'm all ears. What's your information?"

"It isn't so much information as it is a theory."

"That's what we need, Ms. Sinclair, more theories."

Ella was about to justify when Morris waved away her response.

"Oh go ahead, go ahead. You've got 3 minutes to get it off your chest."

Ella swallowed.

"O.K. I think Jason Elderby might know who murdered Katie Merchant. I think perhaps he witnessed it."

"And what makes you think that?"

"The way he's behaving."

Morris stared blankly at Ella. She shifted her weight in the uncomfortable desk chair and continued.

"You see I was thinking, what if these kids are being abused. Maybe routinely. All by the same perpetrator. Perhaps that had some think to do with little Turtino's suicide."

Morris scrunched up his face. "What does Paulie Turtino have to do with this?"

"Well I don't know. You see, that's what I'm trying to figure out. Why did Father Muldoon leave this town in such a rush? I don't buy that he was kicked out for being gay. I know this is a conservative small town but I just don't buy the intolerant shit. It just seems like an easy cover to me."

Morris held his hand out, palm up.

Ella proceeded.

"I think he had a secret and I think that secret may have been pedophilia. Is that a word, 'pedophilia'?"

"Good enough for me." Morris said as he reached under some scattered papers on his desk and pulled out a file. He handed it to Ella.

"What's this?"

"Read it."

She flipped it open and began to skim across the pages. Her attention was captured immediately. She read each word slowly and deliberately in her disbelief.

"...you know I would never reveal to anyone your true anguish, but I can't help praying that you find the strength to ask for the help you need. Your sins are no more vile than those of any man, but they are sins that have a firm grasp on your senses. They are sins which alert your flesh and bring you to climax, and yet sins which destroy your essence, leaving you lost in your smoldering guilt and loneliness. They are boys. Boys who cannot understand nor reciprocate your affections. You will cause them pain. Pain in the pleasure you provide. You cannot justify this.

Ella looked at Morris. "It's eloquent. For a janitor he was quite well read I'd suppose."

Morris nodded. "And infatuated."

"What does he say about this?"

"He's dead. He died in the hospital three days ago. Colon cancer."

Ella read the rest of the letter and the one beneath it before she closed the folder and looked at Morris.

"So you knew he was a pedophile all along!"

Morris shook his head. "No, Ms. Sinclair. I just discovered that little secret yesterday."

"Where did you get this?"

"Dillard. He brought it over here. Said he found it in Muldoon's personal files. I think he was sitting on it until Sikes died."

"The janitor?"

"Muldoon's lover. The man who wrote those letters. The janitor."

"Why are you telling me all this?"

"Because you're the first person who's wanted to know."

116

Ella sighed and looked down at the file resting in her hands.

Quietly she said, "We've got to talk to Jason. Paulie committed suicide. Katie was murdered. That leaves Jason. Maybe more. I don't know. But I almost positive something happened to Jason. The only thing those three kids had in common that I can think of is church."

"Well, give it a shot Ms. Sinclair. Maybe you'll have more luck with the lovely Janice than I did."

Ella glanced sharply at him. "Being a bitch, is she?"

"Not my place to say, I'm sure. Uncooperative is the word I might use. Protecting her young is the phrase she might use. YOU might say she's being a bitch."

"I might indeed," mumbled Ella.

Ella got up to indulge in another of the chocolate chip cookies Chris had brought home.

"Then she told me I should quit interfering in her life. Wasn't it enough that I was sleeping with her husband? She thinks I'm fucking Doug! Can you believe it?"

Chris shrugged non-committally.

Ella looked at him.

"What? What does that mean? Why aren't I getting any support here from you, Chris? You can't think I was fucking him too?"

"What was he doing here at ten o'clock at night, El?"

"Oh Jesus Christ. I can't believe it. Fine. Whatever. I don't know what the hell he was doing here. Maybe he was trying to get in my pants. I don't know and really it doesn't make any difference. The point is Janice doesn't give a shit either, she was just using that as a weapon to fend me off cuz she doesn't want to deal with this."

"What are you going to do?"

"I don't know. Maybe I'll send her anonymous mail containing articles on child abuse and how it can ruin a kid's life if it's ignored. What do you think?"

"I bet she'd like that."

Ella savored the thought of irritating Janice for a moment.

"I was just so infuriated with the way she touted the whole God/Church thing as her excuse for not dealing with it. It drives me crazy, Chris. It just makes me want to slap the God right out of her."

"Is she going to say *anything* to Jason? Even try to talk to him?"

"I doubt it."

Ella stopped picking at her cookie and stared at Chris.

He looked back at her with a suspicious grin on his face and then asked in his mild manner, "What?"

"Thanks."

"For what, hon?"

"For listening to all this. For . . . being here. For being on my side."

Chris reached across the table and ran a finger down her cheek.

"I love you."

"I know. And I love you."

"But?"

"But I think it's more complicated than you think it is."

"You're right. I think it's pretty simple."

"Chris . . ."

"Ella, it's me or him. You can't have us both."

Ella stared at him for a moment. How did they suddenly get on this subject?

"But I can't just shut my feelings off. I can't just pretend like he isn't part of my life. And I don't want to. I can't say I want those feelings to go away. You know, Chris? I love you. But I don't think I want to let him go either. I just don't know that I wouldn't regret that."

"Either way you're going to have to make a decision. And I think you'd better think about all that we've been through together, and the way that we know each other, and how much I want you, Ella. You think about that and you decide."

He stood up and put his mug in the sink.

"I'm gonna go to Boston tonight and stay with Ned. I'll probably be back the day after tomorrow."

He turned and faced her.

"And then I have to know. That's it, Ella. You have to decide."

Chapter 19

Ella closed her eyes. The book in her hand slid gently onto the quilt on her bed. Her mouth opened slightly and her breathing became deep and methodical.

And while she lay resting the forks on the table called out to the forks that were stuck fork end down in the flower pots, "What are you doing in there?"

And they returned, "we are being cleansed, for three days and three nights."

And the knives, disdainful of the forks stuck so conspicuously upright in the soil of the potted plants, said, "Why? That's silly. You look ridiculous."

The table forks turned to the knives and snapped, "it's their tradition. Don't be small minded."

The forks in the pots said, "No. It's not just tradition. It is faith."

"Faith?" The forks on the table asked.

"Yes. Belief. Faith."

"That," said the knives, "is to avoid responsibility."

"What is?" Asked the table forks.

"Faith."

"What do you believe in?" The pot forks asked the knives.

"We don't. We're not afraid of that responsibility."

"What responsibility? You're a knife!" The table forks pointed out.

Ella had been awoken by the arguing in her kitchen and had gone downstairs to see what all the commotion was concerning.

She heard the knives quite clearly for they were rather audacious.

"You are skirting the issue." The knives were telling the forks.

"Well what if you had to decided between two men, both of

119

whom you really wanted. Both of whom give you things you can't get from the other?"

The whole entourage looked at their newcomer.

The knives were annoyed by the intrusion, but the table forks offered her a seat.

Ella sat.

"Well?"

The knives harumphed. "We'd simply let things happen as they may. In the end the best man would win out."

Ella winced. "Thank you John Wayne."

"But what do you call that?" The pot forks wanted to know.

"It's constructive neglect." Answered the knives.

Ella watched the pot forks snicker.

"It's called faith."

"Excuse me?" The knives said.

"You do believe in something: that the best man'll win. That's faith."

"Go to hell!" The knives yelled.

"Absolutely not!" The pot forks yelled back.

Then all hell broke loose and it was all Ella could do to keep the silverware from tearing apart the kitchen counter. It was when the other appliances started to get involved in the battle that Ella got desperate. She grabbed forks and knives alike and threw them all into the sink where she dowsed the obscenity screaming utensils with hot tap water. After several blows to some knives and pot forks with a cooperative spatula the hot water started to take effect and the situation defused.

Ella and Steph sat in "Newton's Coffee and Teas" staring at the Amherst Common. The wind was cold but the sun was shining fiercely, determined to beguile home dwellers into stepping outside for a warm stroll: attempting to deceive those inside looking out: convincing the shop attendants that the final days of autumn were not yet upon them: drawing Ella and Steph ever closer to their steaming cups of milk and coffee.

"All you have to do is decide which one you want."

"That's all is it?"

Steph ignored Ella's sarcasm.

"When I first met Jon I was seeing someone else. Derien was a great guy. But he wasn't going to share me with no other man. I knew that, honey. I didn't even push it."

"Well, how'd you decide on Jon?"

"Oh Ella, I knew. It didn't seem that...I don't know...easy, at the time, but somewhere inside I knew and I just made the only decision I could make."

"I don't just *know*, Stephanie. I keep thinking I should and I'm searching desperately for the instinctual knowledge, but I don't feel it. I really don't."

Ella dropped her head onto her arm and rolled it back and forth.

"Cheer up, girl. We all gonna die someday. Don't let it get you down."

Lydia pulled out the rest of the blintzes from the oven and laid the last batch, fresh from the frying pan onto the top of the heap. Dan took the maple syrup out of the fridge.

"Grab the sour cream too," Bruce yelled from the dining room.

They settled around the table as Bruce finished filling his mother in on the events of the week.

"So, Ella thinks she's figured out Cabbot's theory. But I think we must be leaving something out. We know for sure that Muldoon was molesting kids, probably Paulie among them. But there's no way to prove anything. Muldoon is in the West Indies or something, his boyfriend Sikes died last week and Paulie Turtino hanged himself. Dillard pretends like he doesn't know shit, or maybe he really doesn't know shit, and the Turtinos are too god-fearing to even consider what may have been going on."

"How did you find all this out?"

"We just talked to Ella on the phone. She was in with Chief and I guess he told her a lot of it. We guessed the rest. She confronted Dillard, but he wouldn't budge." Dan said as he helped himself to another blintz.

Lydia shrugged, "But I don't see what all this has to do with Katie's murder."

Dan sighed. "Neither do we. That's why we told Ella to

leave it alone. Unless Muldoon flew in from the Philippines, or where ever he is, to kill Katie it doesn't really matter anymore if he molested those kids or not."

Bruce said, "I think she wants to light a fire under Janice's ass."

"To do what?"

"I don't know. Therapy, maybe. Get Jason into therapy. She thinks Muldoon might have gotten to him too. Ella's big on counseling."

"Well that's California for you. She is from San Francisco. I read an article in Registered about dog therapists in Los Angeles. I can't even afford a weekend in Camden let alone a psychologist for my dog," Lydia scoffed.

Dan nudged her. "You don't have to worry about it, Lydia. You like cats."

"So, for tomorrow read pages 37, 38, and 39."

The bell rang.

"O.K. bye. See you tomorrow."

The sixth graders crowded for the door as Ella sat down at her desk. She had prep period now; time to catch up on her lesson plans.

She heard a shuffle and looked up. Jason Elderby was standing at her desk. He was back in class and looking less morbid. Whether free will, or mother imposed, Jason was wearing colors again. Did it mean anything besides a certain fashion consciousness that he wore black all the time? Who's to say? But blue suited him. Ella considered the preppy T-shirt. Yes, blue suited him. Not the style, but the color.

"Hi Jason. Welcome back."

"Thanks, Ms. Sinclair."

He was mumbling and he wouldn't look at her.

Ella waited a moment before saying, "I know you've been through a lot lately, Jason, so take your time. You're a good student. I'm not going to worry about it much, O.K.?"

Jason nodded at the ground.

Ella waited.

Jason didn't leave. He stood at her desk, head down,

picking at the edge of the desk and digging gently at the grout along the linoleum tile with the toe of his sneaker.

"Ms. Sinclair?"

"Yes?" Ella prompted.

Then he started to cry.

She let him sob for a few minutes. Her hand was resting gently on his arm, giving it a squeeze every now and then. When he started to sputter and quell his tears she handed him a tissue.

"You want to sit down for awhile, Jason? We can talk, or you can just sit there if you like. Nobody's coming in here for another forty minutes or so."

"What happens to people who hurt kids?"

Ella hesitated. "Did somebody hurt you?"

Jason shook his head.

"Did you hurt somebody?" Ella ventured.

Slowly Jason nodded his head.

"What did you do?"

Jason's face flushed bright pink and his eyes welled up with tears.

Ella squeezed his arm again and stood up.

Gently she said, "come on Jas, let's take you down to Mr. Eadly's office."

Chapter 20

It had turned into a long night for Ella. Now, finally concluded, she could crawl into the cocoon of her bed and put the whole disturbing scene behind her.

Instead she stared out her front room window into the rain. It washed down the street in gentle sheets.

Ella's thoughts strayed to Gene Kelley. Who needs an umbrella?

I'll meet you in the rain, Bruce, Ella thought. I'll meet you in the street and we'll walk in the rain.

But Bruce wouldn't be meeting her in the rain anymore. Not to stare at her as he had done before. Not to smile with desire. No glow of affection. They were gone. As quickly as they had come, they had gone.

Bruce had told her so.

"I'm not in love with you, Ella. I was. I think I was. It felt like it. It felt like you were the one. But I don't feel that way any more. I don't know why. I don't know why it went away. Maybe I wanted to believe we could make it work, so I... I don't know."

Ella had stood with her mouth open in disbelief as the words of rejection poured forth.

When she finally did say something, it turned out to be, "I can't fucking believe you're saying this! When the hell did you realize this?"

Bruce shrugged. "I thought about it a lot last night and I guess I figured it out. You're an incredible woman, Ella, but you're not what I'm looking for, not like I thought you were."

"What the fuck does that mean?"

"I do love you, El, but I don't want to spend the rest of my life with you."

Ella stood with a perplexed smile slowly twisting about her lips, hands out, palms up slightly, a squint about the eyes. Slowly she shook her head as if just coming back to life.

"You are so full of shit," she said. "So amazingly full of shit."

"I'm sorry."

She snorted.

"Don't fucking be sorry, Bruce. Just take your bullshit, and your stories, and your lies, and your condescension and get the fuck out of my house and out of my life."

"I don't want to get the fuck out of your life. I want you in my life. I want you as my friend. I need this friendship. It's important to me. I don't want to go back to not knowing you. I love the way you think, and some of the things you say, and what you want, the way you treat people, the way you listen to me when I talk... I don't want to lose your friendship, Ella."

Ella stared at him.

"Fuck you, Bruce."

"Ella..."

"No! Fuck you! Fuck you and shut up! Now, get the fuck out of my house."

Bruce had sighed and shaken his head. But he did leave, without further protest.

That had been that, she thought as she stared at the leaves of the tree across the street jolting rhythmically under the force of the rain. Patter, patter, patter. That's what it sounded like from inside.

She had called Bruce over to tell him what she was feeling, how confusing this all was, to let him convince her to rid herself of Chris, to fall into the well of pleasure that Bruce had promised her. She had been ready to embrace it, without hesitation this time, without any more reconsideration. It was ironic how opposite their decisions had been. Bruce realized he didn't want her anymore just as she realized she wanted to give him a chance.

Patter, patter.

Ella sat up straight. It was pitch black still in her room. She glanced at the clock and registered the early hour. It was shortly after three in the morning. What had woken her?

The telephone shrilled. She groped for it, more to silence the apparatus than to actually speak to the intruder. Who the hell calls at three in the morning?

"Hello?"

"Ella? You've got to get over here, they've arrested my son!"

Janice Elderby's voice was at the edge of control and rapidly losing the battle.

"What? What are you talking about?"

When Ella had dropped Jason off at the counselor's office that afternoon she'd been told he'd be sent home to recuperate. Mr. Eardly thought Jason was experiencing post-traumatic stress and should have more time to recover. All they'd been able to ascertain from the boy himself was that he'd unintentionally hurt another student. He wouldn't say who or how.

"Chief came and got him not two minutes ago! Doug drove behind them. I need someone to be here with Danielle so I can get down to the station."

Ella didn't query any further. Janice's voice was faltering and there was a shiver in her inhalations.

"I'm on my way."

"More coffee?" The waiter asked.

Ella nodded.

"It's the only thing keeping me upright at the moment."

He smiled.

"It's a diner, honey. Coffee is the only reason most of these people show up. That, and the blueberry pie when it's in season. We have our own distributor from Maine and it's the best pie in this part of the state. We've even been written up for it."

He gestured with the coffee decanter toward a framed article on the wall behind Chris.

Chris grinned at the talkative waiter.

"Wow."

The waiter winked at Chris and moved to the next table.

"I think he likes you." Ella said.

"Are you going to be O.K.? You look tired."

"I am tired. After this I'm going straight to bed."

"So, go on."

"O.K. So, they got home at about six this morning with Morris in tow. Their lawyer showed up just as I was leaving but in the meantime Morris filled them in on the charges. I guess there's this young woman in town, Bernice, and she claims she saw Jason going into the woods about the time they think Katie Merchant was murdered."

"How do they know it wasn't Bernice who murdered Katie?"

"I don't know. Motive, maybe. What motive would she have?"

"So they think Jason might have killed her? What motive would he have?"

Ella shrugged.

"I don't know, but he was her age and who knows what might have been going on. Maybe she was going to tell on him for something."

"Like what?"

"I don't know. Shoplifting?"

"Yeah, maybe."

"Well, anyway, he's being interviewed by a social worker right now, and they're going to give him a psych evaluation later. When that's all over they'll release him into his parents custody. He hasn't been formally charged yet, but I have a feeling Chief is convinced Jason killed Katie."

"How are Janice and Doug taking it all?"

"Who can tell? They were both pretty icy to Morris, but I suppose I would be too. And they didn't say a damn word to each other."

"Janice didn't tell you anything?"

Ella shook her head.

"No. But she threw me a glance of... something before I left. Her lawyer was there so it must be pretty serious."

Ella reached across the table and laid her hand over Chirs'.

"I have to go home and get some rest. Will you lie down with me?"

"I don't know. I don't know where I stand with you right now. We've talked about everything else. Have you talked to Bruce?"

"Yeah."

Ella pulled her hand away and stared at her coffee cup.

"Or rather he talked to me."

"What? You're mumbling."

"Yes. We talked."

"Well? What, do I have to guess?"

Ella sighed.

"No, Chris. I'll tell you. I'll tell you what happened and everything we said and all that shit. But not right now. Right now I want to just go home and get into bed and have the comfort of your arms around me. I suppose that's not really fair. Maybe it's more than I should be asking for, but I'm asking anyway."

"That sounds like bad news." Chris said it quietly. "I'm about to get my walking papers I think."

"It's all so simple to men. If you want to make love you make love, if you're in love you're in love, if you're not you're not. It's not so simple. It's work. It's accepting people for who they are and who they let you be. If you find one that lets you be you, then for gods sake, Chris, don't let her go!"

"What the hell are you talking about?"

Ella dropped back against the booth.

"I don't know. I'm tired."

Chris stood up and grabbed the check with one hand and Ella's hand with the other.

"C'mon. Let's go home."

"You really think that's it?"

Bruce nodded.

"Yeah. I do."

Dan looked at his friend with skepticism.

Bruce shook his head.

"I can't live with some of the qualities about her. She wants conflict. Trouble. Constant struggle. I don't. I hate that shit. I want some stability in my life. I'm never going to be able to live like that. It'll drive me crazy. It'll make me unhappy. Really unhappy."

"I thought that's what you liked about her. Hell, when you met her you knew she was all fucked up about this guy. You knew she'd just taken off, split, left her whole life behind her and showed up out here. What the hell did you expect? What did you think that was all about?"

"I thought that was over. I thought she was looking to find something else. I don't know. I thought she was done with that shit."

"Done with it? What?"

"Jesus Christ, Dan. I don't want to spend the rest of my life trying to keep up with her. I don't always want to watch what I say cuz she might not like it and we'll fight, or be afraid that she could just leave me anytime cuz she wants to be somewhere else, or whatever. I don't want to always have to work so hard at it, you know?"

Dan smiled.

"I hear what you're saying, buddy, but I've got my own interpretation."

"I know what you're going to say, Dan. But I really don't want to be with her anymore. I know that. I love her. And she is beautiful. And I would love to fuck her, but I'm not in love with her. Not like I thought I was at first."

"That's cool, buddy. But I think you like her more than you think."

"I wish I did cuz she's great. And she's in love with me, I can tell. I know that's what she wanted to talk about. I saw it in her eyes when she answered the door. I heard it in her voice when she called me. It made me want to grab her and hug her and just forget about it all, not even think about it. But I can't. I just can't."

The temporary silence between the friends was easy. No tension. Bruce was staring out the window of the pub. Cambridge was cute and liberal and filled with attractive college women, but somehow all the charm was lost on him.

"I'm tired. And I feel a little lost with out her, Dan."

Jen reached over and grabbed a beer that the waitress had just set down before them.

"It sounds to me like you're trying to justify being hurt. I think," she held up a finger to prevent Bruce from interrupting her with a retort, "I think, you didn't like playing second fiddle to Chris and this falling out of love stuff is a defense mechanism. That's not to say that you haven't reconsidered the depths of your feelings, but I think you're jumping the gun. You can convince yourself of anything when you get fed up enough, but don't be surprised to get a kick in the ass from a bunch of feelings you thought had disappeared somewhere down the road."

Dan gestured casually toward her with an extended thumb.

"Psych major."

"Yeah, and I've thought about all that. But I really think she's in love with me, and that if I wanted to we could make it work. But there are things about her that I can't live with."

"Bruce," Jen was impatient, "people are who they are. You can't just pick the qualities about people you want to keep. She is the person you adored because of all those qualities."

Bruce scowled.

"I don't have to settle for that, Jen. I can stop thinking about getting married and spending the rest of my life with someone until I meet a woman who's got the qualities I'm looking for. She doesn't have to be perfect, I know that's never gonna happen, but she can get damn close."

"You're going to spend the rest of your life picking apart the people in your life and finding out what you can't live with about them. And there's always going to be something. Figure out what it is that you can't live with about yourself and let your lovers be themselves. Everyone you love doesn't have to be just like you. Fuckin' relax and enjoy the differences!"

Dan and Bruce stared at her.

Dan said quietly, "Hit a sore spot?"

"I'm just so sick of watching you two always trying to figure everything out. Find all the answers. Guess what, boys, there are no answers. There are no answers!"

With that Jen downed the rest of her beer, wiped her mouth with the back of her hand, belched deliberately in Dan's direction and stomped off.

Dan looked at Bruce who's mouth was still hanging slightly open and shrugged.

Chapter 21

The first snow fell that morning, shortly after three. Everyone talked about how early it was this year. It was going to be a long, cold winter with a lot of snow. That was the common belief which bound a village slowly become divided by the unfolding scandal. Ella watched in the grocery store as the North Brooktowners, formerly so friendly, started retreating.

The distinctions between religious sects and ethnic backgrounds which had formerly been limited to those with new money, and plenty of it, were spreading to the groups of townsfolk who had remained relatively unscathed by that previously.

The catholic parish seemed guilty and sheepish around their religious competitors. The Muldoon scandal was resurfacing and the Elderby's were under the firing line. Chief had been digging around, asking questions, and planting seeds. Paulie Turtino's suicide was being re-examined. Every one was wondering and every one was suspicious. Atheists such as Ella and Bruce were the worst of the lot, but they were too inconsequential to bother about. Even Dillard who had been held in such a blameless light had to watch his step. Abstinence required a lot of self-discipline.

Ella noticed the growing tension with dismay. Somehow she couldn't help but feel responsible. She'd been warned to let sleeping dogs lie, but she hadn't resisted the urge to unearth, to get involved, to cause conflict.

"Oh, fuck me. Why do I always have to mess things up, Chris?" Ella wailed.

Chris kissed her neck. They were lying on her bed.

"You can't just ignore a problem, Ella. It's not going to go away. I think you did the right thing."

"You think so?" Ella turned around so she was facing him. "You think I did the right thing?"

Chris nodded.

"I guess that's important. Doing the right thing, I mean."

Chris nodded again, but with slight hesitation.

"Yeah. It is."

"Chris," Ella started.

Chris waited.

"The right thing is to tell you that I'm not hurting over you anymore. I was. Jesus Christ I was! But I don't ache for you like I used to."

Ella looked down, at Chris' chest instead of his eyes.

"I like this, having you here, like this. It's comforting. And I love the sex, but I don't want to be involved with you again. I don't want to get back together."

Chris sat up.

"Think about it, Ella. Think about what you're saying. I was an asshole. And I hurt you. I know that. But you didn't make it any easier. You never told me what you wanted, El. Don't just... I learned my lesson."

Ella sat up and faced him.

"That's not it, Chris. I'm not trying to hurt you for hurting me. I think I'd know better than that. And I think I knew when you got here, maybe before you got here, no, definitely when you got here. I think it hit me the second I opened my front door and saw you standing there; I'm not in love with you. I miss some aspects of our relationship and I definitely miss you, but it's not fair to either one of us to get back together for those reasons. I deserve to be in love. So do you."

Chris stared at her for a long moment and then said, "I am in love."

Ella closed her eyes. "Chris..."

"It's O.K." Chris interrupted her. "I think you're making a mistake. But you know where to find me."

He climbed out of bed and pulled his pants on.

"I'll go back to San Francisco. Call me when you're ready. I'm not going to wait forever and I won't just shut down, but I'll be waiting for you, Ella, for awhile, cuz I think we're right for each other and I think you'll realize that."

"I don't think I will, Chris."

Chris closed his eyes and breathed in slowly.

"Yeah. Well, we'll see."

Chris left for Boston that afternoon. He got a cheap seat on the red eye to San Francisco that night. Ella stood on her front steps and watched him go as the airport shuttle disappeared down Summer Street and turned onto Main. The snow from earlier that morning had turned to slush. It was bitter cold outside and overcast and dismal, just the weather for losing a lover.

Jason sat in the holding cell in the Brooktown juvenile detention facility. He was alone in there, thank God. He had stared at the barren walls for god-only-knows how long. It was driving him crazy. If he weren't so scared he would have cried.

They knew about Katie. Mom kept saying they couldn't prove anything, that he hadn't done anything wrong, but Chief knew. He watched Jason with those suspicious eyes. He gave Jason that look. He even smiled, just a very tiny bit, when Jason said he hadn't been in the woods the day Katie died. But Mr. Clince had said told him that he didn't have to answer any of Chief's questions. He'd said, "just keep quiet, son." So, Jason had clammed up. But when the lady cop had walked in with lunch and said, "it'll be O.K., Jason Elderby. Just keep your chin up," he had wanted to tell her everything. He just wanted to let it all out. Instead he started to cry. He was crying so hard he couldn't eat his lunch and his soup was cold before he even tasted it.

Now he had to wait. He had to wait until Mr. Clince had filled out enough papers to get him sent home. That's what his Mom had told him.

"We'll come and get you as soon as we can, honey. Just be good and don't talk to anyone. We love you."

Mom was pissed. Mom was always pissed. Better than Dad, though. Dad was nothing.

And the whole time Chief watched him, like he knew.

"What the hell have you been telling people?" Janice hissed.

John Dillard sat back in his chair.

"I don't know what you're talking about Ms. Elderby. I haven't told anyone anything. Especially not about us as that would be as detrimental to my position as it would be to yours."

"My husband knows about us, John. He didn't just figure it out, he's too stupid for that."

"Give the man a little credit, Janice. He is protecting his own. Most men figure it out when their woman is being screwed by another man. It's instinct with us. It's our biological programming that makes us want to have every one yet not to share with anyone. He can dick around without conscience, but when you do he knows. He can smell it, Janice."

"What a crock of shit, John! Don't blame your infidelities on your gender, or your biology. You choose your role!"

"I owe to no one. What infidelities?"

"Your infidelity to God, for one. You did take a vow of celibacy."

"My heart is with God. I think that's what is important."

"Whatever, John. I don't give a good god-damn. I just want you to shut up about us. I told you if it ever got out it would be over between us. Well, it's over."

John raised his eyebrows.

"I haven't seen you in over two weeks. I think I guessed that it was over, Janice."

"Two weeks in which I'm sure you haven't been idle."

"Not idle, exactly. But not as active as one could hope. Aren't you supposed to be in Brooktown bailing out your son, anyway? What are you doing here? This won't bode well when the gossips get together."

"Doug wanted to get him. Alone. I thought it would be good for them to spend some time together. That man doesn't even know his own children anymore. Especially not Jason. It's like he loses interest once they reach eight. Daniella has a couple of years left of her father's attention. Or maybe it's different with girls."

Janice was staring out the window. She looked lost.

John's voice softened.

"I'm sorry about this mess, Janice. Is there anything I can do to help?"

Janice stared at him for a moment. Then she shook her head.

"No. No, but thanks."

Dillard watched her as she gathered up her coat and glided gracefully from his office.

Before the door shut behind her John said, "I'm fighting an erection, Janice."

134

"Keep fighting, John."
The door shut.

Doug looked at Jason's determined little face as he edged the car through traffic. When did Jas start looking so much like his mother? Janice was beautiful. He remembered the first time he'd ever laid eyes on her, at that party at the Sigma Nu house sophomore year. She'd been a freshman. A sweet, sexy, determined little freshman. She hadn't fucked him until he promised to marry her. Doug smiled. Determined little Janice knew what she wanted. And he'd wanted the same things. A beautiful little wife, who was pure, his alone. Now look at her, fucking the priest.

Doug glanced back at his son. Jason was under suspicion of murder, Janice was fucking the priest, he was going to be charged with rape if he didn't leave his wife.

No one knew that yet. Just another bombshell to drop on the family. But Doug thought he'd wait for a better time to tell Janice that one of the students he'd been sleeping with got grandiose ideas about becoming the new Mrs. Elderby. It wouldn't stick. She couldn't make the rape charge stick, not this much after the fact. He'd already consulted his lawyer about it. Clince had reassured him that he wouldn't go to jail for raping a college student, but to keep his nose clean from here on out. Doug had tried. And except for the interlude with Sylvia in his office he'd been successful. If he just hadn't seen her damn slip strap.

But he was going to have to tell Janice. Oh, what the hell, she already knew anyway. She accused him that morning after Clince left of sleeping with every two-bit college tease that let him under her skirt. But he'd thrown the affair with Dillard right back in her face. He hadn't been certain about it before, he was now. She stood there gaping at him, saying "What?" and turning red.

Doug's fingers tightened around the steering wheel. The nerve of Dillard, fucking his wife!

Doug saw the tears streaming down his son's face from the corner of his eye.

He glanced over at Jason.

"Son, are you all right?"

Jason's face scrunched up and the sobs burst forth.

"I'm m m m sorry, Da a a a d."

Doug reached over and patted his son's leg.

"We're gonna make sure every thing's O.K., your Mom and I. I promise, Jas."

They pulled up in the driveway and Jason was out the door before Doug had a chance to kill the engine.

Janice's car had pulled up seconds before them and she was stepping out of her seat when Jason threw himself into her arms.

"I did it, Mom! I think I did it!" He yelled.

Then he burrowed his face deeply into her abdomen and sobbed ferociously.

Janice glanced at her husband. Doug looked somber. He was staring at Jason.

Janice waited for him to acknowledge her. When he didn't she turned her attention to her son. She stoked his hair and said, "O.K., honey. It's O.K."

Chapter 22

"So, in your dream the forks in the flower pots were arguing with the forks in the sink?"

"Yeah. And the knives."

"And what does that mean?"

"That's what I'm asking you?" Ella looked at Steph.

"I mean, I don't really see what it has to do with what was going on in my life. I'm getting dumped, after being promised that this is something I can count on, I mean, basically my whole image of Bruce was completely nullified. It was like he was the incredible presence, a picture full of vivid color and beauty, and all of a sudden it rains and all the color gets washed out and now there's just a canvas there with the outline of beauty. But everybody else can still see the color. You see, it's just me that the color got washed away for. It's still a beautiful painting to other people. And it's still hanging on my wall, still with the promise of beauty, and I keep staring at it, but the color is gone, it's just gone. And I feel like it got washed away right after I found the perfect spot for it on my wall."

"Wow. Can you make that analogy again, girlfriend. I think I missed some of it."

"No. I've had too much wine. I don't even remember what I said."

"Something about a painting and color and everybody else."

"Why are we drinking this stuff? It tastes like shit!"

Ella grimaced as she read the label on the bottle of claret.

"It's cooking wine. It's the best I could do at a moment's notice." Steph explained.

"Well pour some more in this glass, woman. I'm almost out."

Stephanie did as she was directed.

"Now, tell me again exactly how he dumped you."

"No. You just want to see me cry. You think it's funny when

137

I cry because my face gets all puffed up."

Steph laughed.

"Well, I do think it's funny when you cry, girl, but that's cuz they're crocodile tears. Honey, if this guy really hurt you I'd be the first one to show up on his doorstep and tell him a thing or two."

"You would?"

"You bet."

"Well, he hurt me, Steph. I ache when I think about him."

"He hurt your pride. And I know what part of your anatomy aches for him."

"No, Steph. Really, I think I could've spent a long time with him. You know, a long time."

"I believe you, Ella. But I know you, you put up a lot of defenses. And there is no way, that in one month, Bruce broke through enough of those defenses to hurt anything but your pride. You suffer from a bruised ego, doll, nothing else!"

"I miss the affection."

"You miss the security. The promise of security."

"It makes me yearn for him."

"If Bruce came back to you, you'd want Chris. If both of them came back to you, you'd leave town. If neither of them is here for you, you want the one that doesn't want you. Whichever one that may be. Don't try and tell me your tastes are discriminating, girl, I know they aren't."

"You're belligerent when you're drunk, you know that, Steph?"

"Yes I do. I know a lot of things. I know that you are changing the subject."

"I'm drunk."

"I know."

"I'm drunk, I'm alone, and my car got towed."

"Your car got towed?"

Ella nodded.

"I parked it in a tow away zone and forgot about it. I walked out of work this afternoon and my car was gone. I hunted it down, though. It's slumbering for the night in a lot near East Brooktown. I have to get a release from Morris tomorrow before I can get it. And I have to pay a hundred and something bucks. Shit."

Steph grinned.

"You lose both your boyfriends, destroy a family unit, set your town on it's head, *and* get your car towed. Rotten luck."

"A very dysfunctional family unit. I don't consider my quest for the truth destructive. It was necessary."

"You don't have to defend yourself to me. I still like you."

"I found out something else, Steph. At the end of this semester they're cutting my job. They're going to combine my class with the other two classes. They lost some more funding and I am low man on the totem pole so my job was the first to go."

Steph stopped drinking mid sentence. Slowly she put her glass down.

"You lost your job too?"

Ella nodded.

"I've got 3 and a half more months of employment."

"If this gets any worse I'm gonna have a vicarious break down."

"I think I'm just going to go teach English in Korea."

"What?'

"Teach English. In Korea. You know, A-B-C-D . . . ."

"Fuck you. Don't get snappy with me! What is this shit about Korea? You're not going to any Korea!"

"Well, maybe not. They haven't accepted me yet."

"Who hasn't accepted you yet? What are you talking about?"

"I told you, teaching Engl . . ."

"I know what you told me" Steph interrupted her, "and you aren't going to Korea. I've finally found a friend out here in Hokey-Finoky who doesn't think church socials are the highest form of culture and who has read some thing other than John Grisham. And you are not turning around and departing for the other side of the world. No way, girlfriend, no way!"

Ella smiled.

"I appreciate your position, Ste . . . "

Steph interrupted again.

"No. You don't appreciate my position!"

Ella started to laugh.

"You're drunk."

"Well what a surprise. I've only had a bottle of wine."

Ella emptied the rest of the second bottle into their glasses.

139

"I've just got to get out of here, Steph. I thought I could do it, but there are too many ghosts. Chris is everywhere. And now Bruce."

"And this is your solution? To run?"

"I'm comfortable with running, Steph. I get restless. Going to places where I have nothing, and I'm alone, and everything is unknown, to me there's something safe about that. It's familiar to me. I know how to do that."

"What about what you leave behind?"

"What about what I discover?"

"Thanks a lot. No wonder no one wants to stay in love with you."

Ella grimaced.

"Touché."

"Well O.K., Ella. But you can come back. Don't stay there because you have to prove anything. Come home if you want to. As soon as you want to. The sooner the better."

Ella squeezed Steph's arm.

"Thanks, girl."

"So, now tell me again what he said? How he dumped you?"

Ella grinned and embarked for the second time on the story of how Bruce expiated their relationship.

Chapter 23

Morris scrawled his signature across the bottom of a release form which looked like a credit card receipt.

"Well, Ms. Sinclair" he said handing it back to her, "you've certainly stirred up a hornet's nest."

"What do you mean?"

"I mean, Paulie Turtino's suicide. I'm surprised you didn't read about it in the papers."

"I'm not in the habit of picking up the Town Crier. I guess I should have. Can you fill me in or is that unethical?"

"Unethical? No secret, Mam."

Ella waited.

"It turns out Muldoon was molesting neighborhood kids. Any one of 'em he could get his hands on. We had a shrink up here interviewing some of the kids he probably had access to. Can't screw around with that stuff."

"Paulie was one of those kids?"

"According to another little kid he spent a lot of time with. They both were. And, like kids'll do, they swore they'd never tell. You know, they were embarrassed and all."

Ella nodded.

"Yeah, I know."

Ella sat down in the chair on the other side of Morris' desk.

"But why Paulie. I mean, why did he kill himself. None of the other kids did."

"I guess you never met Mr. Turtino."

Ella shook her head at the rhetorical question.

Morris looked at her.

"Paulie'd have a tough time explaining that one to his Dad."

"But…" Ella ran a hand through her hair, "it just seems so desperate, suicide. He was so young."

"You've never been that down, eh?"

Ella shrugged slightly.

"I've had some rough ones. But, no, I guess I've never been that down. Plus, my parents... I was lucky. I am lucky."

Morris nodded.

"Good for you."

"What about Katie Merchant? Does she tie into this somehow?"

Morris gave Ella a tiny grin.

"Maybe she does at that, Ms. Sinclair."

"And Jason?"

Morris grinned.

"You're not too bad at this."

"Yeah. I'm big on figuring out people's motivations."

"We all gotta have hobbies."

Ella, Bruce and Dan stood in Mr. Cabbot's Video store at the counter. They were there with her at her request. She hadn't wanted to confront Cabbot alone.

"So you're gonna tell me what you think and see if it's what I think?" Cabbot pointed his stubby finger at Ella's chest. She took an involuntary step back.

"Yes."

"Let's hear it, little lady."

Ella glanced back at Bruce and Dan. Bruce moved up next to her at the counter. Ella breathed deeply, and smiled at him. Bruce winked at her. It was exactly the encouragement she was looking for.

"O.K., I think what happened was..." Ella stopped abruptly and pointed her finger at Cabbot.

"I'm trusting that you even have a fucking theory, Cabbot." She snapped.

Cabbot bared his discolored teeth.

"Don't worry. I always got a theory."

"As long as there's religion and sex involved." Dan edited.

"I think Paulie Turtino committed suicide because he couldn't handle being molested on top of whatever else he was dealing with." Ella said it in one breath.

Cabbot harumphed.

"That's old news. Let's hear it about the murder, sexpot, or stop wasting my time."

Bruce reached across the counter and grabbed Cabbot by the shirt. Dan jumped in grabbed Bruce's arm.

"Call her by her name, Cabbot." Dan snapped.

Cabbot grinned.

"Keep your pants on boys."

He looked at Ella and spoke very deliberately, "Tell me more, Ms. Sinclair."

Bruce let go of Cabbot's shirt.

Dan let go of Bruce's arm.

Ella said, "Muldoon molested Jason. Jason molested Katie. Then he killed her?"

"Hidee ho."

"Why didn't you mention this to Chief? You have a civic duty, you know."

"Don't lecture me, princess. Now get your punk asses out of my store unless you got sompin' else you wanna discuss."

Ella shuddered.

"No. I'm done."

The three friends sat in silence in Ella's living room on the floor. The fire crackled melodically.

Ella took a long drought of her beer, closing her eyes as it slid down her throat into her stomach.

"Good stuff."

"Boston's own." Dan remarked looking at the label.

"Do you think he's right?" Bruce asked.

"What?"

"Do you think Cabbot's right? His theory."

Ella sat up straighter.

"Yeah. I do. I think Jason murdered Katie. I don't think there was anything premeditated about it. I think he just got scared."

"This all doesn't seem a bit out there to you, El?"

"It doesn't seem so out there to me." Dan interjected. "I remember wanting to fuck every thing that walked."

Bruce raised his eyebrows.

"That's changed?"

Dan grinned.

"Yeah. I'm more selective now. I can be."

Ella laughed.

Then suddenly, "Hey, Dan, what's the deal with Jen, anyway? Is she pregnant?"

Dan smiled.

"Nope. No, she's not. And I can't really say that I'm not fucking relieved."

"I'm glad things worked out the way you wanted them to. How 'bout Jen? Is she O.K.?"

"Yeah. She's relieved too. We both realized without ever admitting it that we probably would have wanted different things if she had been pregnant. That kinda puts a strain on a relationship. But we don't have to worry about it now."

Ella nodded.

"Yeah. Relationships are tough." She glanced at Bruce. "They're work."

Bruce smirked.

"I already got this lecture, beautiful."

"Not from me."

"From everyone else. And don't think I haven't been over it in my own head a hundred times."

"What goes on in your head, Bruce, as far as relationships go, is an enigma to me."

"You're no open book, yourself, El."

"Not only am I an open book, I'm annotated and illustrated compared to you!"

"You think this is easy for me? You think you're the only one getting hurt here? You think I don't reconsider every day?"

"Well, don't bother! Don't reconsider, Bruce, cuz I don't want you back. I wouldn't have you back if you came crawling to me on all fours, with your heart between your teeth! I don't trust you. I'm sorry I ever did. It was all just a bunch of bullshit."

"It wasn't bullshit. I thought I felt the things I said. I did. I did feel them. But my feelings changed."

"Well then, you're either shallow or full of shit. Next time take the other person's feelings into account before you go convincing them to believe in you. If you're so shallow that your feelings vanish from one day to the next, feelings that you claimed were the strongest they've ever been, then you should reconsider telling other people about them. Just say to yourself, hey Bruce, I'm a shallow fuck, and this too shall pass."

"Whooey!" Dan breathed. "She's lettin' you hear about it, buddy."

"That's great, Ella. It's all my fault. The fact that you were holding out for your main man to come save you didn't play into things at all, did it? You just worked so hard to make me feel wanted, to make me feel like I was the important one. You were real careful to never make me feel like I was helping you kill time till the love of your life got here. I never felt like an asshole waiting around for you to make up your mind. Yeah, I enjoyed being strung along until he showed up and then not hearing from you for three days. And it didn't hurt me at all to hear you tell me all the time how much you still loved him. You're right, El, I am a shallow fucker."

"You're so good at eliminating your feelings, Bruce. You didn't like the circumstances so you just did away with the emotions. And don't think you're ever going to meet any one that you connect this well with again. It just doesn't happen that often. Some people are amazed if it ever happens at all!"

"Don't you think I know that, Ella?"

"I don't know. I don't know what the hell you know! But you obviously don't know me, or anything about me, or about the way I feel."

She dropped back in her chair and was silent for a second.

Then she said quietly, "And you don't want to anymore. That's fine. That's your choice. But I think it's a shame. It's more than a shame, I just don't have a word for it."

Bruce leaned forward. "I want to be your friend, Ella. A close friend."

"And you probably make a good one. But I don't know. Maybe. Maybe not right now. We'll see."

"But I still get to be friends with you, right?" Dan asked.

"I sure would hope so." Ella smiled at him.

"Well then, it will be so."

He turned to Bruce.

"Wanna go?"

"I guess."

Ella walked them to her front door.

Bruce stood on her doorstep facing her.

"I hope I'll be talking to you soon. I'm right over there you know."

"I know, Bruce."

Ella walked back into her kitchen and gathered up the empty mugs. She stood for a long time with the ceramic in her hand staring at the silent dining utensils resting in the sink. Forks and knives lay this way and that on top of each other. There was no struggle, no debate. They'd found peace, or signed a truce at least.

She sighed and dropped the cups on top of the other dirty dished. She glanced out the back door at the tree, her gently swaying back yard tree, almost devoid of its brown leaves.

Her mind eased over to the other side of town where the Elderby household was trying to live with their sins. No, she didn't want to think about them. They were not her problem. She couldn't save them. There was nothing to save, not by her.

Even San Francisco was feeling an early cold this year. She'd read that in the paper this morning. How fitting, she thought that it was becoming winter.

Acknowledgements

With grateful appreciation for their humor, patience, and hard work, I'd like to thank my publishers, Tony and Mr. Bill, without whom I'd just be another unpublished, misunderstood, mostly ignored, frustrated, why-doesn't-anybody-love-me, (etc.), wanna-be writer.

www.ingramcontent.com/pod-product-compliance
Lightning Source LLC
Chambersburg PA
CBHW071303130626
46556CB00003B/1439